"You don't want me to know about you, do you?"

Annie gave a start when Chris lightly encircled her wrist with his fingers. She stared into the dark intensity of his eyes, fearful of what the question meant. The touch of his hand on her wrist, gentle as it was, brought to mind handcuffs. Then he released her, and she was free again.

"I don't have much to tell," she hedged, just as she had so many other times with so many other people who had attempted to get closer. "There's not much to my life, Chris."

"I think there is," he countered. "I can see it in your eyes."

The certainty in his voice made her uncomfortable, very uncomfortable....

Dear Reader,

Welcome to the Silhouette **Special Edition** experience! With your search for consistently satisfying reading in mind, every month the authors and editors of Silhouette **Special Edition** aim to offer you a stimulating blend of deep emotions and high romance.

The name Silhouette **Special Edition** and the distinctive arch on the cover represent a commitment—a commitment to bring you six sensitive, substantial novels each month. In the pages of a Silhouette **Special Edition**, compelling true-to-life characters face riveting emotional issues—and come out winners. All the authors in the series strive for depth, vividness and warmth in writing about living and loving in today's world.

The result, we hope, is romance you can believe in. Deeply emotional, richly romantic, infinitely rewarding—that's the Silhouette **Special Edition** experience. Come share it with us—six times a month!

From all the authors and editors of Silhouette **Special Edition**,

Best wishes,

Leslie Kazanjian, Senior Editor

P.S. As promised in January, this month brings you Curtiss Ann Matlock's long-awaited first *contemporary* Cordell male, in *Intimate Circle* (#589). And come June, watch what happens to Dallas Cordell's macho brother as... *Love Finds Yancey Cordell* (#601).

JENNIFER WEST
Suddenly, Paradise

Silhouette Special Edition
Published by Silhouette Books New York
America's Publisher of Contemporary Romance

To Mary Clare Kersten,
with many thanks.

SILHOUETTE BOOKS
300 East 42nd St., New York, N.Y. 10017

ISBN: 0-373-09594-5

First Silhouette Books printing April 1990

Printed in the U.S.A.

JENNIFER WEST's

first career was in musical comedy, as a professional singer and dancer. She turned her love for drama to the printed page, where she now gets to play all the parts—*and* direct the action. She lives in Southern California but travels frequently in search of adventures—and sometimes misadventures!—to share with her readers.

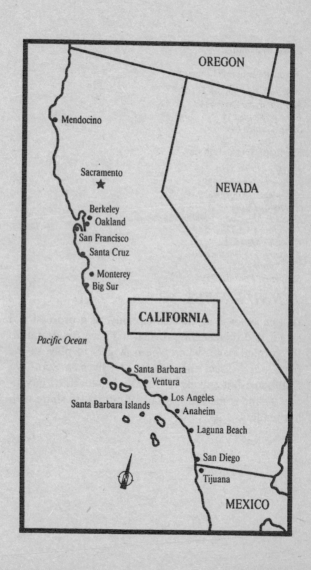

Chapter One

The first bright rays of the new day broke over the Colorado mountains. Like a hurled lance, a beam caught the Volkswagen's mirror, sending forth a sudden flash of light.

Annie started. For an instant her heart stopped, then took up again as she realized it was only the sun. A new day was dawning.

Still, out of habit, she looked around—just in case.

A stand of aspens stood clustered to her left, its leaves shivering slightly as if they, too, had been alarmed. Surrounding the small glade was a carpet of high grasses, speckled with fluffy yellow-headed dandelions, and beyond that, in the distance, she saw the shape of the nearest dwelling, an A-frame house.

Of course there wasn't anyone lurking about. There never was. But for her entire life she had never been able to shake the feeling that someone was following her.

She had tightened her fingers around the thin wood frame. The rest of her body had gone equally rigid. Consciously, she relaxed her death's hold on the canvas she was loading into the van, but the adrenaline shock took longer to ebb.

She began working again, this time with an increased urgency as she loaded each one of the twelve canvases into the van.

Seven months ago, she had gone through the same process, only in reverse. That was in January, and Vail had been a crystal fairyland then, the surrounding mountains majestically cloaked in winter white.

It had been midafternoon when she had arrived. A light snow had just begun falling, and the air had been filled with a soft, expectant hush. The smallest sound had echoed, magnified in the exquisite silence; even her footsteps against the crusted snow had sounded loud to her ears. All she'd been able to think of was sleep. The drive from Texas had been long and filled with a new collection of sad memories of beautiful times ended because...well, because there hadn't been any other way.

She had been dragging herself and her suitcase up the plank stairs to her second-floor apartment, when a patch of ice had snared her.

That's when she had met Kim.

The clatter of human bones and hard plastic luggage had brought Kim out of the bottom story of the chalet and into her life.

"Hi," he had said, grinning as he lifted her to her feet. The fall had done more harm to her dignity than to her physical person. "It sounded like a bear. Maybe two of them. Glad I was wrong."

And for seven months it had been good between them. But now it was mid-July, and there was no more crystal wonderland but instead the soft, rich greenery of summer.

And it was time to follow another road out of another town.

In her pocket was a letter she had written, explaining to Kim what she could. She'd slip it under his door, and in an hour or so he'd find it.

She could imagine him opening the envelope. He'd move to his big upholstered chair, his dark gray eyes following each sad word.

Silently, and not for the first time, Annie cursed Fate. *Why did it always have to be this way?*

She hadn't wanted to hurt Kim; she hadn't wanted to hurt anyone, ever. And yet she had.

Dear Kim,

I hope you'll understand that I had to do it this way, a letter rather than face-to-face. It wouldn't have changed anything to say this in person and would have only made things harder on us both.

By the time you are reading this, I'll be gone. I'm sorry, sorry, a thousand, million times sorry. When we met, we both told each other our "stories." Remember how you had wanted more of a "story" from me, and I told you then that I had none to give you? My life was pretty straightforward, and I didn't hide who I was or how I lived. I'm an artist. I move with my feelings, travel with the wind or the seasons. I always have and always will.

You said you understood. I knew you didn't, not really, but that's what you said then. You said it made me more mysterious, more attractive, having no roots or a past filled with landmarks, like other people. You said you were a man who honored freedom yourself. You even laughed about it. Kim the cynic! You said you were a careless creature of the ski-bum variety, that you lived for the moment. But of course you proved to be much more than the superficial party animal you tried to make yourself out to be.

But I am what I originally told you. And now the seasons have changed, and I'm moving on again.

Kim, you know what we had, how much you meant to me. Remember that, please, and not this ending. And I'll remember you always, and with only the warmest, most loving feelings. Stay well.

Would he hate her, she wondered, touching her fingers to the pocket where the letter was still lodged. Three days ago, he had asked her to marry him.

"Kim! Marriage? Think what it would do to your reputation!" She had laughed in an effort to hide her terror.

Why did he have to ruin everything, wanting to make what they had permanent?

"There would be women hurling themselves off ski runs by the hundreds. Their bodies, along with all their hopes, would be dashed!"

But Kim hadn't laughed. Instead, he had pleaded for the response he wanted. His voice had been tense and worried, as if even then he knew she was slipping away.

"Annie, I mean it. I love you. I want this—to be with you always. Forever. Dammit, don't make fun of this. I've never wanted anything as much in my entire life."

And that night she'd known it was time to go.

Annie glanced at the downstairs apartment with its alpine carvings on the window's shutters. Behind the drawn drapes, Kim still slept.

The last of the canvases had been placed in the back of the Volkswagen van. There were twelve paintings in all, seven finished and five in various stages of completion. When she got to Mexico, she would need to sell the first seven to keep herself going. Her destination was a small town on the gulf, its upscale art galleries catering mostly to Americans who came for brief holidays of deep sea fishing and sunning.

For her, there would be the usual success. Her work was good—better than good; many in the field claimed she was gifted. Although she would never be rich, she could count on economic survival.

But she did not paint in order to pay the electricity bill and the rest. Her artwork expressed feelings that had no outlet in her real life. She poured her very soul into each painting. And she supposed the visual effect ignited dormant feelings in others who reached into their pockets, paying to take the fiery works home.

She secured the paintings, made certain that her few boxes of personal items were all there and checked that her cat's box was padded with an old towel so that Muffin could sleep comfortably. Then she slid the side of the van closed and went quietly back up the stairs to her furnished apartment.

This was always the worst part—the last walk through a place that had been home to her.

Whenever she moved into a new town, she always told herself that it was temporary. It was the same talk she'd given Kim. He hadn't believed her. And maybe that was because she hadn't really wanted to believe it herself.

Each time, leaving was like ripping pieces from her heart.

The bathroom was clean, as was the bedroom. Every trace of her life had efficiently been removed. She closed the drapes, turned and moved quickly into the kitchen to leave the key on the counter for the landlord and make certain the back door was locked.

"Muffin," she called softly, knowing the cat would appear at the first sound of her voice. "Come, pretty kitty...come."

She left the kitchen for the living room, waiting for the cat to appear.

"Come on, Muffin. We've got places to go."

She and the cat had a special bond, as if they both realized the other's independence allowed them to have this singular affection without risk.

But the cat wasn't to be found, not even in a closet. It was as baffling a mystery as it was annoying. In the kitchen, Annie checked both the top and bottom cupboards in case Muffin had crept inside to play or sleep.

Her efforts were rewarded with a soft mewing from beyond the kitchen door.

With relief, Annie peered through the door's window, down to where the gray-and-white cat sat looking up at her with large yellow eyes.

"Muffin—you naughty girl!"

Unlocking the door and swinging it open, Annie bent and scooped Muffin into her arms. Stroking the cat's silky fur, she nuzzled the purring animal against her cheek.

"How on earth did you get out, kitty cat?"

But her hand froze suddenly. Tentatively she moved her fingers over something unfamiliar, something very wrong: a bright red collar—one that hadn't been there that morning—encircled the cat's neck. Happy to have located Muffin, she hadn't taken note of the band that was partially obscured by the thick coat of fur.

Three days ago Muffin's old collar had fallen off, and Annie had been too absorbed in her own troubles to bother getting another.

Now there was a new one.

This one was red, like the previous one that Annie had bought; only this one was obviously more expensive, with the cat's name engraved in a small gold plaque. Kim would never have bought a collar; he believed all animals should be free. No, this gift was definitely not from Kim.

"No! No, no, no..." Annie said breathlessly as she ripped feverishly at the collar's tiny closure. At last freeing the cat from the crimson bond, she tossed the strip of leather aside, and with her heart hammering, quickly backed into the kitchen to safety.

Once behind the locked door, she scanned the outdoors for movement. Nothing stirred. She backed away then, retreating deeper into the kitchen shadows. But still she watched, waiting as she had waited on other occasions, hoping to catch a glimpse of her invisible benefactor.

She stood there for a moment longer, her vigil as always a wasted enterprise, and then fled the apartment with the cat in her arms.

For two hours she kept her eyes trained as much on her rearview mirror as she did on the road ahead. Different cars followed, then passed. New ones appeared. No one was following her; Annie was certain of that.

And at least the incident with the red collar had kept her from thinking of Kim.

But now she did, and hot tears began to trace down her cheeks, accompanied by a regret that choked her until she sobbed audibly, no longer able to be brave and resolute.

As if in sympathy, Muffin hopped from her box into the front seat and snuggled against her leg.

"It's going to be better in Mexico," Annie whispered. "Mexico's going to be great," she promised them both, and pressed her foot harder on the gas pedal, even as the tears fell onto Muffin's soft coat.

Jeff Parker turned his head in slow motion, his light green eyes following the languorous sway of a girl's hips as she passed down the sidewalk by the outdoor café.

"Oh, yeah," Parker intoned breathlessly. "Yessiree...we're talking a definite number nine. Hey!" He made a fist and playfully poked the shoulder of the man seated next to him. "Hey, Farrentino, what do you think? Is she or is she not a nine?"

Beside Parker, Chris Farrentino absently reached for his iced tea. Raising the glass to his lips, he didn't look up. "You're a lecher, Parker." The dry amusement was tinged with the warmth of friendship.

"Give me a break . . ."

"A break? You're thirty-eight. She's only a kid." He put down the glass, its sides sweating beads of cool moisture in the July heat.

"How do you know?" countered Parker. "She could be a hundred and eight, my friend. You didn't even check her out."

"Elementary deduction," Chris said, his eyes still focused on the pages of a police report spread before him.

"What? You've got two sets of eyes? You can read and—"

"Ears, I've got ears."

Parker paused. "Oh. Yeah," he said reflectively, and nodded with understanding.

Reggae music flowed from the oversized radio the teenager carried in one hand. In the other was a triple-decker ice cream cone, its pastel party colors matching her string bikini. A few errant drips had made it to her wrist. Her feet were bare, except for a single copper toe ring. The music was sensual, exotic, teasing the imaginations of those who came to Laguna looking for romance during the summer beach months.

"Gotta hand it to you, Farrentino," Jeff went on, and not without sincerity. "Two years off the job haven't set you back. You've still got the old magic."

"Maybe not." Chris Farrentino flipped through the text of a seven-year-old police report of a local murder, still unsolved. His face bore traces of frustration.

Ironically, it had been Chris's first case for the department when he had signed on as detective. The only reason it had been dredged up from the files again was because a new murder bore certain vague similarities.

Still looking down, Chris shook his head. "You know, Parker, I shouldn't have dropped the investigation back then."

"Yeah? Well, don't wear a hair shirt. You were pulled off."

"Doesn't matter. I should have worked on it on my own time. I was close."

Jeff Parker shrugged. His eyes were on the sidewalk fare passing by, but his mind was not engaged in the flow of bodies. "Maybe," he said, paused thoughtfully and then added, "but maybe not."

"I know I was. Just looking at this stuff, I can feel it all over again. There's something in here . . . something in these pages. I almost have it." He tapped his index finger on the page before him. "But not quite." His dark brown eyes didn't move from the page as he looked for clues that were never swept away by wind or rain or shredding machines.

His eyes were the same deep chocolate color as his Italian grandmother's, a feisty, passionate woman who had come from the rugged, wild terrain of Bari at the turn of the century. Her potent gaze had broken more than a few hearts in Brooklyn, where her family had first settled.

Chris had also, inadvertently, broken a few hearts along the way, but his dark gaze was more purposely employed to penetrate the facades of witnesses and suspects who came under his professional scrutiny. But for the past two years he had been off from work, needing to rethink his life. He had had money saved, enough to allow him the luxury of exploring other avenues of public service, and had devoted his time to volunteering for community outreach programs, working with children's groups, helping the elderly. Catching criminals was important in its own way, but it had felt good to help others in a more elemental way.

The department had kept in close contact with him during his hiatus, and when they offered him his old position back, using Jeff to exert the pressure of friendship, he accepted the invitation to return to work. Now he understood just how committed he was to police work; it was not just a job but a veritable calling.

This was his third week back with the department. He was glad to have challenging cases with which to completely absorb himself. Little by little, the joy of life was returning.

"I thought it then, and I still think it—you're on a wild-goose chase." Parker continued to scan the sidewalk for scantily attired female talent.

In contrast to Chris Farrentino, who bore the sensually romantic looks of his Italian forebears, Parker was fair, with a perpetually florid complexion. When standing to his full height of five ten, he gave the bodily appearance of having been blunted during manufacture. His physique was squared off, as if the original human design had been altered to fit into a box created for a different model. To emphasize the compact impression, he sported a bristled flat-top, a hair-style great on the high-cheeked, strong-jawed male models of *GQ*, not good on Parker. At work people called him "Bull Dog," as much for his determined, unyielding personality as for his sturdy appearance.

"What I think," Parker went on, "what I always thought, was that some nut case did it. You're looking for motive and meaning where what we have here is just your basic, random crime. Trust me on this, Farrentino. It was some weirdo passing through Laguna Beach like all the other drugged crackpots on their way to the border, only this one went over the bend and offed Martin one day. It could have been anyone who got nailed. That's my theory, and I'll stick by it."

Chris remained thoughtful, as if digesting Jeff's rationale. Then he shook his head. "Uh-uh. That just doesn't sound right to me."

"Okay." Parker nodded agreeably. "So just what *does* sound right?"

"Nothing. Yet. But I get this feeling."

"The Famous Farrentino Feeling," Parker crooned expansively, opening his arms wide. "Maybe we ought to get you a turban and a crystal ball."

Chris smiled. "Yeah. So laugh."

"Who's laughing? Not me, pal. I've seen your feelings prove out. Of course, personally I attribute your success rate to luck, whereas my own prodigious record of achievement is a testament to pure genius."

"I don't think I'd sleep easy if I could count only on luck."

"Farrentino, you'd sleep fine if you'd put a woman in your bed." Having said it, Parker paused, stealing a brief, worried look at his longtime friend and co-worker. Then, with a change of tone, he said quickly, "Sorry. Okay, Chris? That was out of line."

Parker stopped talking as a group of twenty or so motorcyclists cruised down Pacific Coast Highway, drowning him out.

"You know how it is. I've got a big mouth sometimes," Parker went on. "And this was one of them."

"No problem," Chris said shortly.

Trying not to think about Parker's unsolicited comment, he looked out across the street, past the steady crawl of cars to the Pacific Ocean. Its rolling blue expanse was broken by the Hotel Laguna on one side, and up the hill to the left the Fahrenheit 451 Bookstore, a favorite haunt of New Age proponents. A startling and stunning mural of gray whales had been painted on the long outside wall of the book shop, which was one of the reasons the café was so noisy. Every other car would slow to take a closer look at the realistically depicted, life-size mammals.

For most patrons, the noise didn't matter. The porch of the cafe was prime people-watching turf. An unending parade of beautiful young bodies—both male and female—in swimsuits and other minimal summer attire made up for the barrage of racket and exhaust fumes.

"Oh, no...oh, no...tell me it isn't so." Parker's voice rose in mock anguish and his fist came down on the table, which he pounded with a schoolboy's glee as another female specimen for his consideration came into range. "All that perfection in one woman. How can such a marvel of nature be? I'm in love again. This one *is* a ten. Look at those legs. Come on Chris, I'm telling you, this is prime stuff.... Will you look at those legs.... I'm dying, man. I'm dying."

But Chris had once again become absorbed in the folder spread open to the side of his plate. Parker's chatter was just more background noise as Chris went back in time seven years to unravel a senseless crime. "The guy's life was completely pure. There wasn't any motive for anyone wanting Jim Martin knocked off. No enemies. No hidden girlfriends. No drugs. No rotten kids. The man was clean as the driven snow." He looked up from the page, seeking a spot in the mid-distance at which to stare unseeingly and contemplate the incomprehensible.

Parker forgot the woman momentarily, his expression showing that he took exception to the notion Chris had just put forth. Chris understood, even welcomed their disputes. That's why they had always made a good team. Although differing in personal styles, they agreed on fundamentals and disagreed just enough to make each think harder.

"Poppycock, pal," Parker said. "No one's all good. No one's that squeaky clean. Everyone's got secrets and dark corners with cobwebs. Don't ever think otherwise. You'd be a damn fool—maybe a dead one."

"Contrary to what you may believe, some good people still exist, some authentic innocents."

"Not even you, Farrentino... not even you are all pure. That is, if we can still count you as part of the human race." Parker's tone had slipped from its former joviality.

A shadow crossed Chris's face. "Don't start, okay?"

Jeff held up his hands, palms facing Chris. "Okay... okay. But I'm your friend." The words bore no hint of apology.

"Then back off. I know the whole routine, so let's not get into it again."

"Look, what I said about having a woman in your bed wasn't cool, maybe. That's real personal territory, sex is. But it wasn't all that wrong to say, either."

"I know what—"

"Laura's been dead for two years. You like facts—Chris, there's a fact."

Chris tensed, defending himself against the pain that rose at any mention of Laura, and particularly when there was the suggestion of resuming a full life without her.

Jeff saw his reaction but went on anyway. "It's okay to look at women again. That's not being unfaithful—it's being normal. It's what men do."

"Don't worry about it. I'm not turning funny on you. Believe me, I look at women," Chris said, fingering the tab on the manila folder holding the details of the Martin murder case.

"Okay. So maybe you do look. But you don't see them. There's a difference."

"I'm doing—" Chris interrupted himself with a sigh. "I'm doing what I can do. So cool it, Jeff. You're my friend—I'm your friend. But there's some stuff that's private. I've got to do things my way. All right?"

"I only meant—"

"Dammit!" Chris exploded. "I know what you meant. I know damn well what everyone means. And you all mean well." He stiffened, fighting an inner rage that had no physical opponent. "I loved her. Can you *get* that? Can *anyone* get that? You don't turn that on and off. Love doesn't work by the calendar, by the clock. 'It's a year, two years, time to boogie again, find some chick and get it on.' Hell, man! It's not like a television set got pinched from my house, or something. This thing with Laura isn't a deal where it's out of sight, out of mind." He lowered his voice as he tried to bring his rage and frustration under control. "Look, I know she's gone, and I know I'm supposed to get on with my life. I've read all the books on death and dying and grieving they've got over here." Angrily, he gazed toward the book store, where the whales swam forever in suspended animation, just as his life had come to seem frozen since the day two years ago when his wife had died after her fight with multiple sclerosis. She had been thirty—just thirty. He had been thirty-one. They had thought they would have forever with each other. Up until she took her very last breath, he thought there would be a miracle, that something was going to happen to save her.

"I even let this over-the-hill hippie talk me into some tome on spirit guides," Chris said, now speaking with less energy. "But it doesn't make any difference. I feel what I feel. And I can't forget her. It's like she's still in me. Or about to come back."

Jeff waited a beat, as if considering if he should say anything more. When he did, he spoke softly, firmly, with compassion. "Chris—she's not coming back. Laura's never coming back. And you've got to go on."

An old, dark green Volkswagen van pulled into the space in front of the café. Chris noted its arrival from the periphery of his consciousness, aware also that a sleek red Ferrari had only just left. Such were the contrasts to be encountered in Laguna Beach. It was an interesting town, a good place to live. A lot of people—Chris included—thought of it as paradise on Earth.

He started to collect the pages of his report, putting them back into the manila folder.

"A twelve," said Jeff. "Bless my soul. It's a perfect twelve. Farrentino, if you're still alive, you're going to fall on your knees with one look at this one. Look at this, Farrentino. Look at her, man, or I'm going to kill you."

Chris looked.

And this time he saw.

Parker was right: she was a twelve. He watched as she came around to the parking meter, studied the instructions, then fished around in her purse for change. Frustration registered on her face.

"Did I tell you."

Jeff's voice broke into Chris's concentration. Feeling strangely foolish and guilty, Chris picked up the file folder. "What?"

"Is she hot looking, or what?"

"She's nice." He looked back at the woman.

"Nice?" Jeff's voice was tinged with disgust.

Reaching for the folder, Chris rose from his chair, careful not to make eye contact with Jeff. "She's a good-looking woman," he conceded, knowing in his heart that he had just made the understatement of the year. "So I'll see you back at the station. I've got a call to make." He dropped a ten-dollar bill on the table, covering his part of the lunch.

"You're hopeless, Farrentino!" Parker called to his back.

Chris didn't necessarily disagree.

To leave, he had to enter the interior of the restaurant and take the front door to the sidewalk. Turning left just outside the entrance, he started up the slight incline to where his own car was parked.

He saw that the woman was still at the meter. Her palm was open with some change displayed, obviously none of it the right denomination. It was a familiar sight in Laguna—tourists lucky enough to get a parking place were rarely lucky enough to have the necessary quarters required for the machines standing sentinel over the rare open spaces.

On other occasions, Chris had stopped and offered a quarter to ease someone's lot. It made him feel good to help. Deep down, there still remained in him a core of innocence.

He felt into his pocket, touching several coins the size of quarters.

He could stop and rescue her from the predicament, making a lengthy and complicated exchange of her nickels and dimes and pennies for the several quarters he had in his pocket. Or, he could pass by, a disinterested pedestrian, and lose any possibility of social interaction.

It had been years since he had picked up a woman, and now the idea of putting the moves on this one seemed preposterous. And yet, as he neared her, a rush of dormant male desire surfaced.

Jeff was wrong to think that he did not have life left within him; he did.

The quarter he had removed from his pocket grew hot in his palm as he strode closer to the woman. Chris guessed her to be in her mid to late twenties, but it was hard to tell about age these days. Teenagers could look like thirty, and forty-year-olds could look twenty-five.

Taken feature by feature, the woman by the parking meter was unusually pretty, her beauty accentuated by the depth of her expression. In a flash of insight he saw her as a young doe abandoned in an unfamiliar glade. Something deep and primal within him throbbed, wanting to comfort, but he knew better than to reach for wild things that were born to make their own ways in the world, no matter how soft or vulnerable—no matter how very, very pretty.

Taller than average, she looked slender and gracefully proportioned in her faded jeans and short-sleeved cropped white T-shirt that came to just an inch above her waist. In contrast to her delicate form, she had a full and abundant fall of sun-streaked hair. Her skin was a tawny golden shade, smooth as glowing silk.

Not only did her physical appearance captivate the imagination, but so did her presence. Even as she stood by the parking meter, she appeared romantically ethereal.

The poetic imagery made Chris prickle with sudden self-conscious embarrassment. He was a criminologist, not a moonstruck adolescent given to flights of fancy.

The quarter, as he passed her by, burned his skin.

In the next instant her voice closed the distance he had put between them, and it seemed as if there had never been any other alternative for him than to stop— as he now did—and to turn slowly, with dread, with hope, and to look with wonder into the amazing depths of her fathomless blue eyes.

"If you might have a quarter for the meter. I've change—" she opened her hand, displaying several coins "—but not the right kind."

Lost in a whirlwind of feelings, Chris hadn't heard the beginning of her sentence. The voice was soft and melodious, yet somehow carried over the din of the traffic behind her.

It was now his turn. "Sure...quarters," he said, and opened his hand, displaying the one he held, ready to be offered before even asked. Immediately, he felt exposed, as if all his previous thoughts related to meeting her were printed in red ink on the coin's face.

"Thanks" was all she said, with a brief smile to further signify her gratitude. There was a quick exchange of two dimes and a nickel for his single quarter.

"Hey, no...that's okay, it's not necessary," he said with gallantry sounding too broad to his ears, and held out the change for her to take back. She would not.

"Don't be silly," she said. "Money's money. Even a quarter. If you've enough of them—" she inserted the quarter into the slot and hit the side lever "—you could park here forever!" This was followed by a soft laugh, but one in which Chris detected a note of sadness.

The meter showed she was good for twenty minutes.

Quickly reaching into his pocket, he fished out three more quarters and slipped each into the same opening. "Just in case," he said with an easy smile despite his inner chaos. "Maybe it's not enough for forever—but it'll give you time to drink a cup of coffee."

"Oh, please..." She started to sort out some more of her dimes and nickels. "I could have gotten quarters from one of the stores—once I had a few minutes on the thing."

"Not necessarily," he said truthfully, refusing the change she offered in payment for his quarters. Either he was losing his mind, or she was the most beautiful woman he had ever seen. "The merchants can get a little testy at this time of the year—with everyone hunting down quarters for the machines."

"Oh. Yes. I guess it would be kind of a pain," she said. "Anyway..."

The blue eyes held him like a steel vise. He did not want to be let go. He wanted to stay with her. He wanted her to stay—to stay forever. He would put millions of quarters in the machine if he had to.

Suddenly she was saying, "Thanks. That was really nice."

"No problem," Chris said with self-assured charm.

"Well...thanks again," she said, gazing up at him for one long, last moment, before she started to ease away from him.

And then she was crossing the street, her back to him, and he was watching the easy swing of her hips, and the long, tapering legs. "Farrentino, you jerk, that was one incredible woman you just let slip away."

The voice was his own.

And so was the pain of loneliness as he set off, striding up the hill to his car.

Chapter Two

The double lines of cars from each direction moved slowly, inching up the gentle incline. Annie moved briskly across the busy thoroughfare, slipping between a Porsche and a convertible Suzuki Sidekick, then stopped in the center of the street, waiting for another break in the traffic.

It was safe to jaywalk; no one here was in enough of a hurry to drive over you to get to a meeting on time. This was the Southern California coastline where only the sun and the surf reigned supreme.

Above Annie, a flock of gray and white gulls swooped low, crying out raucously. Vaguely, she followed their course as they careened toward the Pacific.

Taking her next chance, she moved into a clearing and made it as far as the next lane, before a pink Cadillac with white-walled tires and gleaming tubular mufflers blocked her path.

Stalled in her progress, she looked up again at the
birds, following their path as they made for the open
sea. There was something wonderfully free about them,
and she thought of how she might paint the scene,
bringing in the mural of the whales and the palm trees
off to the right, along with the cresting waves of the
Pacific. Then she would add the people, rendering them
as small stick figures, insubstantial against the vast
scope of nature.

Laguna Beach would be a good place to paint, she
considered wistfully. It might even be a good place to
live. But such a thing wasn't possible.

Still, drawn by the yearning for permanence, she
looked behind her to the place she had just left. She
noted that the man who had donated his stash of quarters to her parking meter cause had also moved on.

With surprise, she realized she was unaccountably
disappointed not to find him still there. The thought
was silly. They were no more than passing strangers.

She searched the crowded sidewalk for the light blue
of his polo shirt, and found him swinging along up the
hill, a strong, masculine shape with shining dark hair
ruffled by the sea breeze. For an instant her attention
remained fixed on him. Then a horn blared.

The light ahead had turned to green, and she, too,
moved on, winding cautiously between the cars.

But her thoughts returned to the man.

At first glance, she had found him to be extremely
good-looking: tall, dark, muscularly lean with the
flawless olive skin of people from the Mediterranean.
Probably he was of Italian descent, although just as
possibly Greek, the kind of man whose dramatic looks
brought to women's minds the potential of romantic

adventure, and generally underscored a glib and self-interested personality.

But the dark eyes meeting hers had radiated a surprising degree of natural warmth, and the smile was likewise genuine. Along with these potentially heartbreaking qualities, he seemed to possess equal degrees of self-assurance and tentativeness.

For an instant, she had thought he might try to hit on her. But again, she had been wrong.

He hadn't asked her where she came from. That would have been his logical opening. The question would have led into a casual conversation about her, or the area, which, in turn, could have led to an invitation to have a coffee or ice cream, or to take a tour along the boardwalk.

It would have been an easy and acceptable move for him to personalize their chance meeting. After all, it *was* summer, and this *was* the beach, and the season was primed for such impromptu romance.

Actually, she respected him for the restraint. It meant he had scruples. Some woman, somewhere, was very lucky. And of course there had to be a significant other in his life—he was young and good-looking and male.

She thought of Kim. Would he have turned to someone else already in an attempt to forget her? She couldn't blame him if he did. Although their friendship had been deep and she missed him now, she had never loved him with her whole heart.

She had reached the opposite side of the street. Veering left on the sidewalk, she passed a bookstore, another shop and finally came to the gallery, which was the sole reason she had stopped and parked the Volkswagen. Earlier, she had passed the display window as she'd cruised Pacific Coast Highway looking for a reasonable hotel.

Muffin had taken ill while they were headed south on the freeway toward the Mexican border. Within two hours, they would have crossed from the United States into Baja, where she and Muffin would find a few months of peace, if they were lucky.

But with the cat in pain, Annie's only recourse had been to interrupt their journey. She sought a vet at the nearest exit, which turned out to be Laguna Canyon Road.

The prognosis had not been good: feline female problems. An operation was necessary, followed by a recommended week of recuperation, periodic checkups and a final visit.

The painting in the gallery's window had caught her eye only because the traffic was moving so slowly that she had time to study the scenery. At first glimpse she had thought she was mistaken. Then she hadn't wanted to believe her eyes.

And now her legs felt like lead weights as she moved with dreaded anticipation and an accompanying undeniable fascination across the few remaining feet to stand before the window in which the single painting was displayed.

Standing before the clear plate glass, all thoughts of the man and Kim and Muffin and Mexico dissolved, as did also the summer's day.

There was only the painting and the feelings it evoked.

The canvas she stared at was large, the landscape an oil painted in the soft, hazy tones one would associate with a dream or a distant memory. The impressionistic style contrasted sharply with the subject matter—a large commercial bus, its entire body covered by a scene of rolling hills, mountains, streams, animals, trees, birds, and over all of it, the firmament with a constellation of stars flowing like a river into infinity.

The painting was entitled *Starstream*.

Starstream: the name inscribed by the artist along the side of the bus.

Starstream: the folk-rock band that had risen to cult status during the late sixties, the lives of its members coming to a sudden, tragic conclusion one early dawn when the bus had gone over a cliff on a hairpin turn.

Starstream: her painting; her heritage.

The last time she had seen the bus, she had been eight years old. Her name had been Canaan then; the Annie had come later, out of the need to avoid the publicity linked to her famous parents after their deaths.

There had been another reason for the name change, one far more serious. The police had claimed that the accident was rigged, that Starstream's drummer, Corrie Bonner, the only member of the band not on the bus when it crashed, had tampered with the steering mechanism. There was conjecture that Corrie was crazy and vengeful, that he might seek out Canaan and kill her, too.

That last time Annie had seen Starstream, she had climbed up the three metal steps, clutching her doll in her hand, ready to take her usual place in the special seat her father had made higher so that she could see out the windows. But Michelle, her mother, had called to her, telling her to come down. She would not be going this time, Michelle had explained in a low, rushed voice. She was to stay in Bakersfield with Michelle's friend. They would be back together soon, Michelle had promised. Michelle was going to come for her. But it was a promise her mother had been unable to keep. Starstream became a memory Annie found too painful to recall—except for one occasion when she had dared to paint the past as she remembered it during her eighth year.

And then it had become necessary to forget again, and she had left the dangerous souvenir from her past in a Florida town. She had thought she would never see the painting again.

Suddenly, even as Annie watched, a woman in white slacks and a hot pink blouse lifted the oil off its hook and removed it from the window.

Only then did Annie become aware that she had been crying. Discreetly, she blotted the wetness with the back of her hand.

The woman had twisted around in her effort to move the painting out of the display case. Catching sight of Annie, she hesitated and smiled slightly. A brief look of concern crossed the woman's face as she saw Annie's distress.

A moment later Annie passed from the street into the gallery.

The woman looked up from the sales counter, behind which she was busy with some papers. She smiled as she saw Annie enter. "Hi," she greeted her. "I see it affected you, too."

Annie must have looked puzzled.

"The painting in the window," the woman clarified. "My Starstream masterpiece. It's fantastic, isn't it?" The woman had moved around the barrier to stand near the canvas, which was now propped against the front of the counter. "It has that effect on just about everyone who looks at it. A very powerful piece of work." She nodded, as if agreeing with someone else who had made the claim. Turning her attention back to Annie, she said, "You know the story?"

Annie stared at the painting, her heart hammering. This was a mistake. There would be questions now, discussion, danger. She wanted to flee. But she couldn't. The painting would not release her from its spell.

Annie nodded. "Didn't the bus belong to the group Starstream?" Her voice quavered slightly.

"Right. I'm telling you, *everyone* remembers it— young or old. It's like with the Beatles. The music touched a chord, something primal, and no one forgets. Anyway, that's what good art is. It grabs you way down deep."

"No one forgets." The phrase drew her closer to the painting. She moved slowly, reluctantly, as if approaching a dangerous and unpredictable beast.

"Their music was about simple, timeless things. Things that last," Annie said agreeably, feeling that a comment was required.

"Oh, tell me about it!" The woman laughed, waving her hand. "You can't step into an elevator where they don't play 'Shining Through' on the Muzak system." The art dealer moved closer. She stood beside Annie, looking down at the painting. "It certainly was tragic. The whole band dying in that accident."

"Not the whole band," Annie heard herself saying. She was immediately sorry. It was dangerous to get into these discussions. She had only wanted to look at the painting again, then be on her way.

"Oh..." The woman paused for an instant. "You're right. The drummer lived, didn't he? The guy who did it."

And there was the little girl, too. But Annie didn't add this piece of information. "How did you get it?"

she asked abruptly, her eyes fixed on the image of the bus.

"Oh." The woman's face brightened. "You know, it was crazy, really. My husband and I were in Key West. We went to an estate sale there and found it. The benefactors were in Europe. I guess they were rich enough as it was and weren't interested in sifting through the furnishings of the man who had died. Anyway, I saw the painting, made an offer and grabbed it before one of those vultures from Palm Beach could swoop down and snatch it. I only put it up for sale two days ago. Would you believe it sold the first morning? I'd give anything to get my hands on the artist," she said, shaking her head in regret. Then she laughed. "We'd both be rich, and she'd be famous."

The woman introduced herself then. Marge Briskin was her name, and she owned the gallery. She appeared to be in her early forties. A pretty woman with taffy-colored hair, she was energetic and sunny. She had done some painting herself, and showed Annie one or two of her own pieces, which were hanging in the back of the gallery.

They weren't very good, but Annie kept her opinion to herself, saying only, "Nice colors."

"You mean nice colors and mediocre work!" Marge laughed. "Don't worry. I know what's good, and what and who isn't. As an artist, I'm stinko. Doesn't matter. I like to paint anyway. And someone who wants a decorator piece will buy both of mine. These will hang over a sofa and someone's dining room credenza, and the owners will be as happy as if they'd hung Rembrandts."

"Who bought the Starstream painting?" Annie asked abruptly. It was like asking about a child given up for adoption, and she averted her face as she waited for the answer.

"A local developer bought it. Great taste, *and* big money to complement it. The two rarely go hand in hand," Marge joked disparagingly.

"Lucky man," said Annie, feeling strangely unsatisfied by the answer. She wanted to know more. What was the home like? Did he have children? Would the painting be something special, or would it be placed in a back bedroom, in a room where the blinds were always drawn? What did he feel when he looked at the bus?

She moved back to the front of the gallery to look once more at the Starstream canvas.

"I don't know if I did right," said Marge Briskin, following her, "but I let the Starstream piece go for far less than I could have gotten."

"Really?" Annie couldn't help but be curious. She wouldn't ask, though.

She didn't have to. In the next breath Marge Briskin confided, lowering her voice as if someone were there to overhear, "He got it for only $8,500. Can you believe that? It's worth at least double, maybe three times that, if it were in New York or Palm Beach. But he's a good customer, and I let him have it under the proviso that he seriously consider a couple of the bronzes in the back room. Anyway, I'm no shark. Money's always been secondary—maybe because I'm an artist."

Annie continued to stare at the oil.

"Are you interested in anything in particular?" Marge asked. "I have some good seascapes by a new artist."

Annie shook her head. "No—no, I just saw that in the window." She looked up at Marge. "I was just curious."

"If I could only find the artist. Canaan. That's all I know—the name on the canvas. Strange name, isn't it?"

"Promised Land."

"What?"

"That's what it means—it's biblical. Canaan was the promised land. It's from Genesis."

"Well, this promised land's completely vanished—there's no trace of the artist. I've checked everywhere. Someone this good wouldn't have given art up. Unless they died. I suppose that would be possible." Marge Briskin shook her head. "I'd hate to think it, though. What a waste."

"A lot of things happen," Annie said, wishing that she could for once bare her soul. "Anyway, thanks for your time. And good luck with your work."

Marge grimaced. "Yeah, well, don't look for me in the Guggenheim."

"It was nice meeting you," Annie said, and gave the painting a parting glance, then began to edge her way to the front entrance.

"Nice meeting you, too," Marge returned, her voice bright with genuine friendliness. She followed Annie halfway across the room. "Stop by again. Are you from the area?"

The question the man should have asked. "No. Just passing through."

"Oh, well . . . too bad. But pass through again! Anytime."

It took Annie an hour to finally give in to the fact that unless she wanted to spend all her cash on a bed and starve to death, she wouldn't be able to afford any of the local hotels whose rates were sky-high in the summer.

She had decided to leave Vail at a time when her funds were at their lowest ebb. She had always had a casual relationship with money—the artist in her, she supposed—and rarely saved much more than she needed to live on.

For an additional fifteen minutes, she sat in the Volkswagen bus, thinking of what to do.

Marge Briskin looked up in surprise as Annie pushed her way through the front door of the gallery, barely managing to hold on to the four canvases she lugged with her.

Sheepishly, she said, "Well, I'm passing through again—I guess a little sooner than I thought I would."

Marge helped her with the paintings, her expression interested as she saw what Annie had brought into the store.

"Well, well, well . . ." Marge said, appraising the oils with narrowed eyes. "What have we here?"

"The work of a starving artist-turned-peddler."

"You being one and the same?"

"I suddenly find I'm in an embarrassing financial situation."

"Welcome to the club," said Marge, her attention still trained on Annie's paintings.

"No. I mean *seriously* in trouble," Annie emphasized.

She told the story of Muffin's operation costing her an unexpected $1,500, inclusive of X-rays and drugs and vet charges. "If I could have made it to Mexico, there wouldn't have been any trouble about the money. The peso's devalued, and there's a gallery there, where I'm sure I would have been able to sell these before my cash ran out."

"I'm sure, too," agreed Marge. She lifted her gaze from the four paintings, and there was a look of admiration bordering on awe in her eyes as she said, "*You* did these? Really? You?"

Annie laughed. "Yes."

"My God," Marge said, shaking her head, "you . . . are . . . good."

"Thanks. So . . . would I be good enough to have you buy them? I need to find a place to stay until my cat's able to travel. There's nothing available in town that would leave me with money to eat. And I don't want to go too far off. I'll need to be close to the vet."

Marge shook her head. "Listen, I'd really love to help you. Honest I would."

"But."

"But I'm not in a position to buy anything outright just now. Mostly I work on consignment," she added apologetically. Then pausing, she went on with an enthusiastic lilt, "Wait a minute. I may have just the answer. We own a little rental up in the hills, my husband and I. It's no palace, mind you. And the people there last were a little eccentric in their choice of paint for the inside, but if you want, I can let you have it really cheap—if you'll clean it up. I haven't had the chance to get to it yet, and it'll cost me to have a service come in, anyway. In the meantime you can leave your work here on consignment. Believe me, this'll all sell," Marge said, turning back to the four canvases. "I guarantee it'll sell."

It wasn't until Marge had handed her the key to the house, that Annie noted that the Starstream canvas was gone.

"Haverstrom's wife came by for it ten minutes ago. I wish these paintings of yours had been here. She would have loved them."

The disappearance of the painting from the gallery bothered Annie the rest of the afternoon as she cleaned the small house. In accidentally coming upon the Starstream oil, she had momentarily reclaimed a brief, shining part of her life. She felt its absence now as a loss.

Her temporary lodging had turned out to be a homely white frame structure, its architecture dating back to the forties. There was a small front porch, the planks slanting down toward the narrow blacktop street that wound, twisting and curving, up from Pacific Coast Highway into the hills, lush with Southern California's semitropical vegetation.

But in spite of its dowdy form, the house had its own strange appeal. Three vibrant shades of bougainvillea blossoms, the branches twining like gay feathered boas around its squat shape, whimsically decorated its exterior. From the inside, a small patch of the blue Pacific, otherwise obscured by trees, could be glimpsed from the single wide front window.

Marge Briskin hadn't exaggerated when she had said the past occupants had strange decorating taste. Annie found the interior of the house to be a humorous conglomeration of wild color combinations.

The bathroom walls were chartreuse with purple molding, the bedroom an ice blue with a navy ceiling on which white clouds had been painted. And in contrast, the living room and kitchen were a startlingly stark white paint.

It was close to five o'clock when Marge Briskin stopped in with additional cleaning supplies.

The early evening seemed unusually heavy and close. Marge commented on a storm blowing in from Hawaii as she placed detergent beneath the kitchen sink. "Anyway, we could use the rain."

Annie's own mood had not lightened. She had not stopped thinking about the oil. Handing Marge a cold diet soda, she said, "This man who bought the painting...the Starstream—"

"Haverstrom. Hal Haverstrom," Marge said, standing. She placed the cool can against her brow, rubbing it back and forth across her forehead.

"Do you think he'd sell it—for a small profit?"

"To you?"

"Well, I don't have the money right now. But I could get it in a few months. It's something we could negotiate if he'd consider selling it to me."

Marge shook her head. "Anyway, it's not a question of money with him. The painting's something...well, I guess, you'd have to say it's something personal. His daughter died a couple of years ago. Twenty-eight years old—around that age. Multiple sclerosis. The girl was his only child, and the sun rose and set with her. I guess Starstream was her favorite group. She was an all-out fan. You know how that is. So the painting represents something to the parents—a piece of their daughter...her feelings. Who knows exactly?" Marge shrugged. "Forget it. Knowing Hal, I don't think he'd sell *Starstream* to anyone."

"The painting means a lot to me, too," Annie said with more passion than she had wished to show.

Marge raised her eyebrows. "Wow. Another heavy-duty fan?"

"Something like that," Annie replied. She followed the remark with a quick, false smile.

Marge Briskin looked at her thoughtfully for a few moments. Then, she said, "Okay, why not? It can't hurt to try, can it?"

She walked to the dining room table, where she had dropped her day planner. Flipping through the address pages, she found his telephone number and wrote it down.

Annie took the piece of paper. Already she felt lighter. "Thanks, Marge. Again."

"Well, don't give me credit where it's not due. I'm not totally philanthropic. I happen to have a hidden agenda of my own. I might be able to get a sale out of this. My advice is, don't pounce on him about the Star-stream oil. Let that evolve.... First, tell Hal you're an artist and that I'm carrying your work. He knows me well enough to trust my judgment in giving you his number. Tell him that I think he'd like your paintings. A lot. Tell him that."

"You're great," Annie said.

"And another thing, just between you and me, the Haverstroms are loaded to the gills. Plus, his wife's crazy for art. So go for it."

Annie did.

On the phone she didn't mention the Starstream oil. Instead she did as Marge Briskin had suggested, touting her own work as something the Haverstroms might like, and mentioning that Marge was representing her.

They agreed to see her.

An hour later she was led into the Haverstroms' expansive living room. The multilevel house was built into a steep incline high in the hills overlooking the Pacific. The interior was open and spacious with large windows looking out over the city below.

"My husband will be right in," Liz Haverstrom explained apologetically. She was an attractive, dignified woman with salt-and-pepper hair. There was an air of reserve about her, or perhaps it was the strain of the family's tragedy that had muted her personality.

"He's downstairs with our son-in-law, bringing up some old photo albums from the storeroom. I'll hurry them up. Please make yourself at home." She smiled warmly and gestured to the long sectional sofa covered in a white silken material, then left Annie on her own.

Curving gracefully, the sofa was inviting. But she turned her back on it, drawn instead to the Starstream painting that was already positioned over a cherrywood credenza housing an entertainment center.

She was studying it, locked in dark thoughts, when a male voice sounded from behind her.

"Amazing, isn't it?"

Annie turned to face her company.

She had been about to smile, about to say politely, "Yes, an excellent piece of work," or something of that order; instead, her intention dissolved, and she could only stare.

In turn, the man across the room seemed every bit as surprised by her presence.

"Well," he said, coming forward, his dark eyes shining with amusement, "it's the lady with the nickels and dimes."

"And the man with the quarters."

"This *is* a coincidence." He followed the statement with a smile, and added, "Sounds like something out of an old movie, doesn't it?"

"One of those English dramas."

"Oh," he said, feigning disappointment. "And I was thinking along the lines of Cary Grant."

As he approached, his steps soundless on the thick, white pile, she took in the difference in his attire from this afternoon. Now he was more formal, at least by the relaxed standards of Southern California. His shirt was a soft white raw silk, and the tailored slacks cream colored, and he wore beige loafers. The white against his skin showed off his dark coloring to excellent advantage.

It would be impossible for any woman not to be attracted to him. Annie found herself admitting that she was no exception.

He stood before her, an arm's reach away, smiling. For an instant neither of them said anything, and she knew that he, too, had been studying her just as closely as she had scrutinized him. She doubted that very little passed by this man without his notice.

In deference to the humidity, she had chosen to wear a bare-backed black sundress. She was vain enough, female enough, to wonder if he liked her in it.

She had swept her heavy abundance of hair to the top of her head, where she had anchored it in a fluffy and careless knot. Now, feeling the man's eyes on her, she self-consciously brushed at her veil of bangs.

"We haven't met formally," he said, extending his hand. "Chris Farrentino." His smile was white and perfect.

"Annie. Annie Adderly," she said, and smiled back. The strong male hand was warm in hers as his clasp lingered. Even after she had withdrawn her fingers, she continued to feel the pressure of his grip.

"You're an artist," he stated. "Liz told me. Oh—they'll be up in a minute. Hal and I were—" And he broke off. "They had some things to put away," he finished. The brightness in his eyes dimmed.

At that he turned and walked toward a small built-in bar on the other side of the room.

"That's okay," she said, following him with her eyes and wondering at the change in his mood.

"I'm having Cutty on the rocks. What can I get you?" he called behind him.

"Wine. White, if you have it."

"Coming up," he said. "Liz likes Chablis. Is that—"

"It's fine," Annie said.

The back of the bar was mirrored, and she could see his face clearly. He was an incredibly sensual man, not only by appearance but by manner. If it was possible to combine both elegance and raw animal appeal, then Chris Farrentino had managed the trick.

Within her, a physical longing arose. It was accompanied by the desire to connect with a man who might end her wandering, and to whom she might bring a world he had never imagined.

In the next breath, as if burned by the feelings she had for him, she looked away.

The attraction was useless. For one thing, what she craved was mankind's eternal fantasy. Life was not that way; life was a compromise, the ideals never realized. Starstream's songs had been about the absolutes of life: the total love, the complete joy, the notion that unicorns and virgins met in enchanted forests. And those gentle souls of Starstream, who had propagated the utopian myths, had perished off the side of a cliff just before dawn one morning, the victims of a crazed murderer.

There was life's reality, for you.

A random glance brought her attention to rest on a handsomely framed photograph on a nearby table. The picture looked several years old—a wedding photo—of a beautiful young woman and a handsome young man. The man was Chris Farrentino. The woman had to be the deceased daughter of the Haverstroms, whom Marge Briskin had mentioned. They looked stunning together, obviously very much in love at the moment the lens had caught them.

Inexplicably, Annie felt sad, even jealous of their happiness.

She turned, looking up from the photograph just as Chris came toward her with the drink. His dark eyes flickered, and she knew he had seen her studying the picture. She felt as if she had been caught prying into his personal life.

The moment was awkward for them both.

"I—"

"No—it's okay," Chris said bluntly as he handed her the cut crystal glass. As if to shut her out, his eyes had deepened in color to an opaque obsidian. "Laura died two years ago—two years and one month ago, to be exact." He glanced down at the photograph for a prolonged moment, then looked back at Annie. The dark eyes shone brighter now, a veil of moisture responsible for the shine.

"I'm sorry," she offered feebly.

Chris nodded. Abruptly, he turned and moved to the plate-glass window, where the lights of the beach community had just come on.

"It's a good picture," he said stoically.

Annie followed behind him. "She was very beautiful," she said softly, compassionately. She stood next to him. They both looked out, their eyes on the city below.

"Yes. She was very beautiful. Laura was a lot of things. All of them good." Then he paused, and as if not really meaning for Annie to hear, he said, "You're beautiful, too."

He said it without even looking her way.

"Thank you," Annie said simply. The compliment came as a surprise. It was obvious by the emotion he displayed—or rather tried to hide—that he still loved his wife.

He looked down at his drink, swished the two ice cubes around in a spiral. "I'm trying to get over her—still trying," he qualified. "We all are—Hal, Liz, me."

Annie nodded, understanding far more about the grieving process than he could ever suspect. She also realized he had just managed to tell her that he was not emotionally available to any other woman. "It must have been an awful time."

"Strange, the things you learn about life. And death. Life doesn't really end when someone draws their last breath. The dead still exist even when they're gone."

"Yes," Annie said quietly. "Yes, I know that."

"I didn't," Chris Farrentino said. He turned his face, smiling without any pleasure as he looked down at her. "That's my business, you know—death."

"The funeral business?"

This time he laughed. "Nothing so lucrative."

"Then, let's see ... you must be a killer?"

He laughed again, and the mood between them lightened by several degrees. "I work the other side of the fence. I'm a cop—a detective. Homicides are my specialty act.''

Behind them, they heard talking, and both turned to see Hal and Liz Haverstrom framed in the wide opening to the living room. Both stopped, as if suddenly frozen, their gazes taking in the scene of Annie and Chris standing beside each other.

Annie felt she had intruded upon hallowed ground.

For a moment, it was uncomfortable, then Hal said, "So—you're the wonderful artist, are you? I took the liberty of calling Marge after we spoke—just to be on the safe side," he added with a laugh. "She said you were something very special. A real talent.''

The room looked as if it had been designed around him, the white showcasing his vibrant coloring, the blue carpet accentuating his eyes. He was tanned and well built, with almost completely silver hair. As a younger man, he must have done serious damage to a few female hearts. At middle age, perhaps the mid-fifties, he was still a stunner.

The kinetic force of Hal Haverstrom's personality energized them, and for the rest of the evening the developer dominated their conversations, establishing a subject, cutting it short to break in with a new topic and leading that to its own conclusion, one determined by Hal Haverstrom's whim.

Annie was amazed by him. In spite of his commanding nature, he did not sacrifice charm, nor did it seem artificial when he said that he loved her work and would definitely make a purchase. The only thing he wanted, however, was an opportunity to view some of her other finished paintings.

In contrast, Liz Haverstrom was kind and sweet, a calming counterbalance to the firebrand she had married.

Only Chris Farrentino seemed uncomfortable. He shifted in his place on the sofa, jiggled his foot, fiddled with the swizzle stick in his crystal tumbler, and sometimes seemed to be in his own private world.

A few times Annie had caught him watching her with a look signifying attraction, and yet when their eyes met by chance, he immediately severed the connection. Either he would look away, or the brown eyes would suddenly lose their previous liveliness.

She tried to ignore the chemistry between them. Men were low on her list of life's priorities. Still, it was almost impossible not to respond to the dark eyes gazing over her body.

She switched her train of thought to finances. *That* cooled her off.

It was reckless, and Annie knew she didn't have much of a chance, but she made her offer to purchase the Starstream painting, explaining that the group represented an important part of her childhood.

"It's more than a piece of art to me," Annie said to Haverstrom, choosing her words with care. She needed to convey the strength of her feeling, yet she could not under any circumstances give away the secret behind those feelings. "The group... Starstream... was a part of my life. They were..." She stopped then, suddenly afraid but compelled to give voice to the truth, she said, "They were *me*."

"I understand," Hal said. "that was exactly the way our Laura felt about Starstream. It's why the painting is so special to us. I hope *you* understand why it wouldn't be possible for us to part with it."

As Annie and Hal discussed the painting, Chris felt himself splitting in two.

Ridden by guilt over his desire for the beautiful woman he had met only a few hours before, he also could not deny his physical need. So badly did he want her, in fact, that he had to leave the room twice on false pretexts to make calls to the police station.

He was on his third Scotch, and it would have served him well to blame his confusion on the alcohol, but he had too much honesty in him to settle for such a lame excuse.

And yet he had every reason to be confused. It was cruelly ironic that both Laura and Annie were so attached to Starstream.

As Annie Adderly spoke of her feelings for the group, it was almost like listening to Laura. Images of the two women kept merging and separating in his mind. He wanted to preserve the sacred love for his wife, wanted to cherish it and protect it, to keep it untarnished in the private shrine of his heart. And yet—God help him!— he needed this other woman who was beautiful and sexual and vitally alive.

Hal said something, and Annie laughed.

Chris stole another glance her way. The object of his desire and dismay sat on the sofa, innocently unaware of his inner chaos.

He wanted to look away but couldn't, the urgings of his libido holding him fast.

The tanned legs were modestly crossed, yet leading his thoughts into immodest places.... And the hint of her breasts, rising just past the crescent of the bodice, which he could imagine ripping off her in one savage motion, made the need grow stronger.

He shifted his position, and Annie stood just then, smoothing the folds of the black cotton dress over her legs.

Hal and Liz rose, too, and dizzy from his fantasies, so did Chris.

"Guess I'll be taking off now, too," said Chris, breaking into the parting banter. "Early day tomorrow. I'm back on the Martin case," he added as an aside.

Hal's blue eyes widened. Annie thought he might have even caught his breath.

"Jim Martin's case?" Hal verified.

"Yeah. Strange, isn't it?"

"But it's been years . . ."

"There was another murder recently—a land appraiser. There were certain similarities . . . not much to go on, but then the case never had anything. So it's worth a try." Chris was acutely aware of Annie standing near him.

"Good," said Hal with enthusiasm. "If you could get that son of a bitch who killed Jim—"

Liz put her hand on her husband's arm, quieting him. Hal had turned a pale shade, calling to mind the color of bleached bone. A small nerve twitched on the right side of his temple, further testimony to his emotional upset.

Chris understood.

Jim Martin had been Hal's business partner. They had started out together and had enjoyed a relationship that was close to that of brothers. When Jim had been murdered, it had been a terrible blow to the Haverstrom family. That was another one of the reasons that Chris had wanted to unravel the case and let justice be done. The case was personal. In fact, it was when he had interviewed Hal about Jim's murder that Chris had met Laura, home from her Eastern college.

"I plan to," said Chris with a firmness that he honestly felt.

There was a round of goodbyes and promises that Annie call the next day about showing her work. Chris was to remember next Thursday night's dinner. Liz promised Chris lamb with mint sauce—his favorite, she told Annie as a special aside, as if the disclosure signified something infinitely more important than what a man liked to eat. Annie recognized the woman's loneliness.

Chris walked with Annie in silence to the front of the house. It frightened her that she felt something special for this man; he was different from any other man she had known.

Their cars were parked on opposite sides of the street. Her green Volkswagen van was closest. It wasn't going out of his way to walk her to the driver's side, and he waited while she unlocked the door.

The night was very still except for the chirping of insects. A small breeze ruffled the branches of the nearby eucalyptus trees. The sharp, astringent odor from the long, flat leaves mixed with the sea air to form a heady perfume.

"Well, I'd better take off," she said.

"A storm's coming," Chris said at the same time, their statements overlapping. They both laughed.

"I heard," she said, feeling awkward because she knew he was gathering courage to talk about more than the weather.

They were standing close, she by the door, her keys in one hand, her other hand holding a small clutch purse. She had left the four paintings with the Haverstroms. When she brought by the other oils the next day, they could all be viewed at once.

Chris was looking at her, his dark eyes catching the light from a nearby street lamp. An inexplicable tenderness came over her for this man who radiated strength and gentleness and sorrow. She wanted to touch the side of his face, to run her hand along the high cheekbone, to trace the ridge of his nose and press her fingers softly against his lips. He was a beautiful man.

"I was wondering—" Chris began tentatively.

"We'd better not," she said softly, turning her face slightly from him.

"Better not what?" he asked.

She looked back at him. "What you were going to suggest."

"I was wondering if it was going to rain," he said, sounding mildly offended. Then with a small, amused smile, he went on. "Okay, you're right. Why? Why won't you see me?" he asked.

"Chris…" It was the first time she had said his name. It felt comfortable on her tongue. "I'm not staying here in Laguna Beach," she said. "I'll be leaving in a week."

"A dinner doesn't constitute a contract for a lifetime commitment. At least it didn't when I used to date. Maybe things have changed since then."

Annie shook her head, also smiling. "I'm just different, that's all."

"I'd say difficult, anyway."

"Let's compromise and say 'cautious.' Look—it doesn't take a crystal ball to tell that you aren't ready to see anyone yet. You're not over your wife."

"I've got to go on."

He said the words as if by rote.

Annie sighed. "Ah, and I'm going to be your guinea pig."

"No!" he objected strenuously. "Well, all right. But take that as a compliment. You're the first woman I've wanted to see since Laura. There's probably a few people in this town who'd build a shrine to you. Look, I know a great place for seafood—which also happens to have one of the most spectacular ocean views in California."

"I'm going to leave in—"

"I know. In one week. I can handle it. But maybe you can't," he said. "Maybe I'm just too irresistibly attractive and you're afraid you won't be able to leave," he joked.

"Maybe," she said, not joking.

"So there's no problem. We both know the score, and as far as I can tell, it's a perfect match. You're going to leave anyway, and I can't involve myself emotionally with anyone yet. So we've got no problem."

"No problem," Annie murmured without confidence.

"I'll pick you up tomorrow around sunset. And be hungry," he said.

He opened the van's door for her, shut it securely and was walking to his own car when she called out, "You don't have the address."

"All in a day's work," he returned, looking over his shoulder. "If I can discover where the skeletons are buried in other people's closets, I can find your place."

Annie knew it was just a joke—the skeletons in the closet bit. But what he had said frightened her. She had to be crazy to go out with a detective. What if he looked into her own closet?

Chapter Three

 W hat do you think?'' Chris asked with the eagerness of a small boy, though his physical appearance told a story of a man certain of himself. "Is this everything I said it would be?" He watched Annie intently, expectant of her reply.

Annie could have said yes immediately. But she had been looking at Chris, lost in a dreamy analysis of his own special beauty. The call to reply jarred her from the pleasant laziness of her private thoughts.

"Everything, and more," she murmured, and to herself silently added, "much, much more."

At her reply, Chris nodded, his face relaxing into an expression of satisfaction. "Good. I wanted it to be something special for you."

"It's totally magnificent," she added with more vigor this time. But the scenery, spectacular as it was, had little to do with her feelings: "magnificent" described the company she kept. She had never been as happy in her entire life as she was now. Everything Chris did—from something as simple as pulling out her chair to what he said—was unique and real and solid. Never in her life had she felt so protected, so fussed over, so precious to anyone. The experience seemed somehow surreal, and she cautioned herself, as she always did, not to be swept into a stream of hopefulness that would evaporate at the next bend.

They sat on the terrace of Las Brisas—in English, "The Breezes." The sun was setting over the Pacific, its vibrant colors glowing in the evening sky. The restaurant's outdoor patio was filled to capacity with beautiful people in various kinds of attire from work suits to beach cover-ups. Music played softly over hidden speakers, mixing with and diffusing the laughter coming from patrons seated at the curving, gaily tiled bars and individual wrought-iron tables. A glass windbreaker wrapping around the confines allowed an unobstructed view of the scenery beyond the terrace, where roses bloomed and the lush greenery of California's semitropical vegetation grew. Near where Chris and she sat, a fire pit blazed.

She was on her second margarita, Chris on his second Corona beer, complete with a lime shoved down the bottle's narrow throat. He had ordered a selection of hors d'oeuvres ranging from a tangy guacamole dip to oysters on the half shell, to a dish of scallops in a garlic butter sauce, served with French bread.

"This is hard to believe...." Annie said almost in a whisper. With her eyes she continued to scan the scene. "That anything can be this beautiful...this perfect..." Quickly, to distract herself from her overwhelming feelings of happiness, she bent her head to the thin red straw in the iced margarita.

When she looked up, Chris was watching her, his dark brown eyes glistening in the firelight. For an instant she thought he understood what she had tried to hide from him. But then, in the next moment the belief gave way to cynicism, and she decided that the intelligence behind the dark eyes was more than likely a product of the light's angle.

"I really wanted you to like it," he said. "Hometown pride, I guess."

Annie tried to concentrate on what he was saying. "It must be wonderful, living here."

Chris looked past the glass windbreaker, where in the distance three surfers rode the long curl of a wave toward shore. One tumbled off his board. For a moment his form was lost in the foam.

"Can you believe it? I used to surf, too. Those days seem like another lifetime." The surfer reappeared, his head bobbing as he swam after his board. Chris turned back to her. "Ever tried it?"

Annie laughed. "Surfing? No, that's one thing I've never thought of doing. Never one of my things."

"What, then?"

"You mean sports?" she qualified, but a pretty cocktail waitress, her long, tanned legs revealed by a slit more than halfway up her thigh, edged past them with a full drink tray, and Chris's mind was claimed for an instant. At least his eyes wavered.

He blushed slightly when he saw he had been caught. "Obviously a possible suspect in one of your cases," Annie commented, smiling. Unaccountably, she found herself experiencing a thorny prickle of jealous possessiveness.

But what did it matter to her? She was leaving in a few days, going on with her life in Mexico. Chris Farrentino would be another pleasant memory, no more, no less, by the time she got to Mexico. But as she looked across the table, she no longer felt serene.

"Occupational hazard," he said, seeming truly embarrassed to have been caught in a display of libidinous male curiosity.

"Casing the surroundings?"

"Yeah. Something like that." He paused to collect himself. "But . . . getting back to our conversation . . ."

"Yes, getting back."

"What interests you? Hobbies . . . sports, other things? I want to know everything," he ended pointedly.

Their gazes met, and the moment grew serious. Annie looked down, breaking the intimacy. Reaching for a tortilla strip, she scooped up some avocado dip. She didn't bring it to her lips, though; instead, she held it before her, staring at the thin, crisp wafer as if not knowing what to do with it. She gave a start when Chris lightly encircled her wrist with his tanned fingers.

"You don't want me to know about you, do you?" he said.

Annie stared into the dark intensity of his eyes, fearful of what the question meant. Was this just some dating rap? Or was it something else? The touch of his hand, gentle as it was on her wrist, brought to mind handcuffs. Then he released her, and she was free again.

"I don't have much to tell," Annie hedged, just as she had so many other times in the past with so many other different people who had attempted to get closer.

"Okay, so you don't have a bio big enough for a major motion picture. But you've got to have been doing something on this planet. Tell me what there is."

Annie sighed. She stalled for time, sweeping her fingers through her hair. "Really, there isn't anything very interesting, Chris."

"I can handle boredom."

She took a breath, then began, leaving out the early years and jumping to where it became safe and anonymous. "I studied art. Here and there. No major schools, no master teachers. I learned what I could from a lot of different sources and tried to develop my own style. Some people say I have—myself, I'm never satisfied. So that's it basically. You see?" she said ending with a slight shrug, seeking affirmation of her opinion.

"Sounds impressive," Chris returned.

"Oh, come on. Impressive? A lot of people study art in second-rate schools—no big deal."

"Your art *is* a big deal," Chris said, challenging the image she projected. "I'm no connoisseur, of course, but it's been said among certain circles that I've an eye for what's beautiful." He smiled slightly, letting it be known that he spoke of more than statues and canvases.

"Must be the Italian in you."

He laughed. "I like to think I carry the genes of da Vinci..."

"Oh, I see."

"I'm glad," he said, smiling smugly.

"Wonderful roses," Annie said, attempting to lure him into safer territory now that humor had distracted them from her personal history.

But she was not to be so lucky. He had not forgotten the thrust of his questioning and continued with, "So why didn't you become rich and famous? Your work's good enough—I'm sure of it. Just by the way Marge talked about you—and Hal and Liz, too. They know good from mediocre. They also know good from great. It was pretty clear they thought your paintings were better than merely good."

Annie looked down, both pleased and worried by his comments. "I moved around. Never really thought about developing a following. I just enjoy painting, painting for the sake of painting, you know? There's not much to my life, Chris. Like I told you."

"I think there is," he countered.

The certainty in his voice made her uncomfortable. Annie reached for her glass.

"I can see it in your eyes," he said, studying her hard.

She lowered her lashes.

"I can tell from your smile," he continued. "It begins sometimes—then fades. I'm no psychologist, but I know a person who's seen some bad times in her life."

"Now I know why you're a detective," she said too quickly, then laughed to hide feelings that would have driven him to probe more deeply. In the back of her mind, she always heard the words of the executor of her parent's estate, the attorney who was responsible for her name change. *"From here on in, you're Annie. Canaan doesn't exist anymore. If anyone finds out the truth, you never know.... There's a killer out there. It could mean your life."* Quickly she finished what was left of the frothy mixture in her glass.

Chris also laughed. "Sorry," he said. "You're right. I'm giving you the third degree. Habit. The nose keeps on working overtime."

And with great relief to Annie, the subject changed to the gray whales, which used the ocean corridor by Laguna to migrate. There were sharks in the water below them, too—the large, bad kind that attacked surfers during the summer. It was hard to believe that such romantic surroundings could hold such treachery.

Chris explained that an excess of sea lions, attracted to the kelp beds, had, in turn, attracted the marauding man-eaters. Public alerts had been posted for bathers to beware of venturing too far out of the shallows.

"But people never think anything bad can happen in the summer, not in a town like Laguna. It's too beautiful. At least on the surface," he said.

The sky darkened with surprising speed, but the magic remained in the sea air and in the flickering candlelight. Annie also believed that nothing bad could ever happen to anyone in this town.

They dined inside, then walked off their dinners with a stroll along the beach, reached by taking what seemed like an endless flight of wooden stairs from the cliff to the sand.

The moon was high, almost full, but not quite. Some dark, ragged clouds stretched across a lighter-hued sky. There was the same heaviness to the air as the night before, but the storm had not shown itself in any other way.

"Storms don't usually hit the coast during the summer months," Chris commented. "January, February, those are traditionally our months for rain."

"It turns cold here?"

"Cold? Hey, the temperature plummets all the way down to seventy degrees. Sometimes we even wear sweaters. Still, you never know. A lot of strange things can happen in life—so maybe rain in July will be one of them. In my line of work you start to realize the arbitrariness of life early on. And then you live with life's surprises and twists as best you can."

Annie listened, fascinated as he continued to speak about his work. He had a passionate sense of honor, of what was right and wrong, and was immensely stubborn, although she knew he would have preferred to use the term *committed*.

She even spoke a little about her own love of art, keeping everything she said fairly impersonal, and Chris listened as intently to her comments as she had to his own.

They walked side by side, carrying their shoes. They laughed often, and allowed themselves extended periods of comfortable silence.

Twenty minutes into their walk, a light breeze took up, coming off the ocean.

Annie had worn another summer dress, this one a pale blue with thin spaghetti straps. The air was a warm caress against her skin. The gauzy material of the circular skirt was wrapped about her thighs, and the curving fullness of her breasts was outlined against the dark of the night.

She was acutely aware of her body, and equally aware of Chris Farrentino walking beside her.

"I don't want this to end," Chris said abruptly.

He was much taller than Annie, making him over six feet by at least a couple of inches, for she was close to five seven, and she had to look up when she sought to make eye contact.

Now she saw that his attention was fixed on the lights of million-dollar homes dotting the cliffs and hills of Laguna Beach.

"It feels right," he said. "This feels good, and I don't want it to end." But the words were half lost when a large wave hit the shoreline.

"Can't hear..." Annie had to shout.

"I said . . ." Another large wave broke.

Chris turned, and in a spontaneous urge to make her understand, he took her in his grip and shook her slightly. "I said that I don't want this to end!"

As if jolted by an electric charge, they both drew away. Chris dropped his hands, his face registering the turmoil of someone who had inadvertently committed a social error.

"Sorry," he said. "I didn't mean to . . . I guess I got a little carried away by the moment."

Annie understood the feeling. Disoriented by her own strong emotions, she could think of nothing to say as she followed Chris with her eyes. He had stepped away from her, as if to promote sanity between them. His form shimmered in the moonlight, like some ethereal god placed momentarily before her.

Then, in a voice that caught once before she forced out the confession, she said, "I love . . . tonight . . . too."

He smiled then, recognizing in her nervousness that she was equally affected by the night, by him. It was a smile of a thousand candles.

For an instant she felt that she, too, might leap into his path and shake him by the arms, yelling that it wasn't the ocean or the moonlight or the tequila that had made their time together special. It was being with him that had made the difference, and that she never wanted to be parted from his company.

If he had tried to kiss her then, she wouldn't have stopped him. Neither propriety nor her need to protect herself from any deeply felt emotional involvement would have prevented her from physically returning the affection she felt at that moment.

But he didn't attempt to kiss her—just as he had not pushed himself on her during their initial encounter at the parking meter. In a way it was maddening—now that she was ready to take chances; but, in another way his keeping his distance was a relief.

They walked again, this time in a silent march of retreat from their momentary passion. Conversations began haltingly and adhered strictly to neutral subjects, until Chris suggested they take in a jazz club in Corona del Mar, the next small beach community up the coast. It wasn't until 2:00 a.m., closing time, when truth had to be faced between them.

He drove her home, to the address he had obtained from Marge Briskin at the gallery. They didn't speak much on the short ride. The tension in the car was enough to set the air humming.

"Thanks," Chris said when they pulled up before the small white house.

Shadows emphasized the high planes of his face, giving him the sculpted look of a Grecian statue. Annie had to force herself to breathe evenly.

"It was—" He broke off, seeming to search for the correct words. "It was the best night I've had in a long time. A long time," he emphasized.

"Me, too," Annie said softly. She looked down at her hands in her lap, then out the window. She didn't know where to look, or what to say.

Chris studied her for a long moment, then nodded in response to some thought. Coming suddenly to life, he said energetically, "So let's get you up to your door. As I recall, you've got a furry patient to visit tomorrow morning."

The walkway was at an ascending angle, outlined in flowering oleander shrubs standing six feet tall. Mock orange bushes and low-growing night-blooming jasmine filled the senses with perfume.

"I feel as if we're being watched," Chris said as he moved with Annie along the narrow walkway.

Annie stopped suddenly, her body rigid. "What?"

Chris paused, taking in her reaction. At first he laughed, seeing the stricken look on her face. Then when he finally understood that she was genuinely afraid, he said, "A joke. That's all." He tilted his head toward a collection of stalky bird-of-paradise plants.

Annie shook her head, laughing a little. "I thought maybe you were serious," she said.

At the front door Chris took her key. "You should get a dead bolt," he said. He unlocked the door and handed the key back to her.

"But I'm not staying," she said softly, almost guiltily. "Remember?"

Chris hesitated, then nodded. "Yeah, sure... I remember."

But she could see he had forgotten; it was so easy to forget things you didn't want to have happen. "I had a wonderful time, a really wonderful evening," Annie said, as if to make up for spoiling the mood by the reminder that such times were not to be a part of either his life or hers.

Chris nodded again, withdrawing into himself.

"So," Annie went on, wishing that things didn't always have to be spoiled, "I guess we should call it a night. Thanks again..."

Chris stopped her as she turned and closed her fingers over the doorknob. His hand was warm and gentle on her shoulder. "What if we didn't?" he suggested.

She didn't turn around. "Chris..." Her tone indicated refusal.

"No, wait. Don't say it." He guided her around until she half-faced him. "I understand you're not that kind of a girl." They both smiled at that. "But, see, I'm not that kind of a guy, either. It's just that . . . hell . . ." He looked heavenward, shaking his head in self-mockery. "It's like I said—I don't want this to end. Not yet. I was thinking of . . . coffee?"

Annie studied him for a moment. "Coffee would be good," she said cautiously.

Chris stayed in the front room, while Annie went into the kitchen.

Hers was a lot like so many of the places built years ago in the forties. They had been constructed as summer retreats by the affluent of Los Angeles who would take the long ride to the south-lying beach communities.

As he walked around the room, studying what there was of the inelegant furnishings, one ear trained on the busy sounds coming from the kitchen, his glance fell on the ugly sofa, a faded tweed daybed.

A heat arose in him, and he turned away, moving quickly to peer out the front window. He attempted to think of other things, less troubling things—like the Jim Martin murder case.

For a few minutes he was able to lose himself in the serpentine details of an investigation that had yielded nothing for seven years, but that he had never been able to categorize as unsolvable, even after he had been pulled off it.

He had met Laura then, and now Laura was gone. He would like to finish off this case. It represented a period in his life that he wanted to be over.

Annie had put the kettle onto the stove, but had forgotten to turn it on. This she noticed only after she had taken out the cups and put them on saucers, which turned out to be salad plates instead.

It was hard to think. She was giddy with happiness.

A couple of times she had stolen looks into the living room, where Chris looked out the front window. In contrast to her agitation, he stood very still. She thought that maybe he would suddenly announce that he was tired and leave.

That would be best, she told herself, because nothing would come of this. It couldn't.

And in the next beat of her heart, she felt that if he left now, it would be a tragedy on the scale of the last scene of a grand opera.

When the tea-kettle whistled, she filled the cups with instant coffee—all that she had on hand—and brought them out on a small tray, along with sugar and milk and two spoons. That in itself was strange, because she took her coffee black, and she remembered that at dinner, Chris did, too.

She entered the room, stopping just inside the doorway. "At last," she announced. "Sorry for the delay. I'm not used to this kitchen."

At her voice, he turned. His eyes were dark yet luminous in the pale golden glow from the one table lamp near the sofa. He seemed to have an instinctive, masculine knowledge of a woman's body as his gaze traveled the length of her form. She felt herself flush from head to toe.

"Thanks," he said, taking his cup from the tray when she had reached him. He looked down at the coffee, and for that she was inordinately grateful.

Chris took a slow sip. The coffee was strong and hot and, he hoped, sobering. The vision of Annie outlined against the kitchen light had just about done him in. Her legs were long, and except for bikini panties—exposed as a darker shape beneath the translucent fabric of the dress—she was unclothed. Her breasts were high and round. As he'd stared, the nipples had become distended. His desire was instantaneous and powerful. He wanted to arouse this woman, to merge with her, to feel—and yes, maybe to possess—every molecule of her being...

Now he found himself afraid to look at her.

"Is it too hot?" she asked, standing close.

He almost laughed at the ironic aptness of her remark.

"No—it's fine," he said.

"Would you like to go out? I saw you staring out the window—the view's wonderful from the corner of the porch."

He let her go before him, and passing near, he caught the scent of her perfume, clean and sweet and fresh...and totally feminine. He trembled again slightly, and reminded himself that he was there merely for company, and to forget about anything more.

They stood close, each with cup in hand as if afraid to put them down, even when empty. Below, the lights from the city shimmered.

Chris listened as Annie said something, laughing lightly. But he couldn't concentrate on her words. His need swamped every thought, every concern as he reached forward, touching her hair with one hand. Then abandoning his cup to the porch's ledge, he took hers and placed it there, too.

"Chris..." she said in way of protest, or perhaps warning, as he drew her around to face him. But he didn't look into her face. He could not let her see his need, which was too raw, too honest, too vulnerable. Instead, his eyes lowered, he brought both of his hands to her face. Cupping her chin, he traced his fingers lightly against the delicate jawline, then tangled his fingers in her hair and finally looked into her eyes.

Then, seized with another savage wave of desire, he brought his lips against her eyes—the salty taste, the scent of perfume, flowers, her, the sea air and the soft, brief flutter of long lashes against his face closed out the world.

And she did not push him away.

Instead, she yielded, bringing her mouth to his, pressing into him until he gasped and had to pull away, fearful that he might completely lose his mind and with it, all control.

He felt himself ready, straining with hard need to join with her now. He fought against himself.

But she made his retreat brief and impossible for, touching her hand to his face, she urged him to return to her. Almost stumbling, he walked her back to the shadows of the porch and, positioning her with her back to the house's white siding, pressed his torso against hers, grinding out a safe but agonized fantasy of the reality he sought with her.

She moved her hips sensuously to the rhythm of his own, and he gasped. "Annie . . . don't do this if—"

But, looking into her face, he became only more entangled in the passion, and he moved his hand from her waist to the smooth, rounded curve of her hip and buttocks. The fabric bunched between his fingers, and hardly aware that he was doing so, he gathered the folds of material between his fingers, working it ever upward until the skirt was lifted completely from her legs.

Their mouths were attached, tongues entwined. At her small cry, he gasped for air and shook his head, wanting to devour all of her.

Both of the thin spaghetti straps had fallen and were now draped over her slender arms, and it was nothing for him to edge the bodice down. Her breasts came to view, and for an instant he could only stare, captured by her beauty. She trembled, and he looked into her face, questioning her feelings.

"Chris...I...I don't..."

It took every bit of his willpower and sense of honor to say, "I'll stop if you want..."

Suddenly, she returned to him, kissing him, bringing one of his hands to cover a breast. With his lips he found a nipple then, and she watched him, moving her own hand slowly against the fabric of his slacks, along one leg to the hard swell pressing against her.

He fumbled with his belt buckle, managing it finally, then the zipper. It was an easy task to slide away the fabric of her bikini pants. He could take her inside now, to the sofa...or into a bedroom. But he didn't want to. He wanted this...in the open air with the scent of the sea air and the flowers, with the shadows covering them, and the moonlight filtering through the branches of trees that hid them from the outside world.

"Like this...?" he asked anyway.

"Now...oh, Chris...here, now..." She trembled again, shivering from passion and desire.

And with a thrust, he pressed himself urgently against her, losing himself to the ecstasy of the silken smoothness of her flesh. He had forgotten—God help him!—he had forgotten it could be like this!

For the first time in so long, he felt himself drowning in the familiar pleasures of being a man with a woman. He had forgotten...every day, it had been this way, the pleasure, with a woman, with Laura he had—

Laura.

And it was over.

The moment of possibility canceled by a name.

Chris drew himself away slowly, the air sharp and cold where an instant before there had been the fire of Annie's flesh.

He could hardly look at her. He was devastated with shame, with guilt, with a fury and a crippling helplessness. "I'm sorry..." he said, meaning it.

He moved out of the shadows, holding Annie's still form, and leaned against one of the posts supporting the porch's overhang. His legs, a moment before having the strength of a stallion's, had become weak, the ground unsteady beneath him.

Annie watched him. She was glad for the darkness as quietly she let her skirt fall to cover her legs and drew the dress over her bare breasts. She felt the slow wane of her desire and the lingering ache of regret.

"There's nothing to be sorry for," she said. "Sometimes... sometimes things just happen."

She had wanted him—still did—but she also understood. It had been shortsighted of her not to realize that this would have been the end.

"Or they don't happen," he said dryly. "It's not you," Chris explained. He looked back briefly, his eyes filled with helpless confusion.

"You're just not ready yet."

"No. I guess not. I'm sorry," he repeated, looking away so that she could not see his expression. "I thought I was okay. I felt like I was. And then..."

"Old memories?"

He gave a short, ironic laugh and shook his head as if to clear away unwanted images. There was a tinge of anger to his words as he continued. "I know the score, I know all the psychobabble about moving on in life.

I've even read books about the grieving process. But I felt—'' He broke off and fell into silence.

"Unfaithful."

He sighed. "Maybe I'm different. Maybe I'm the one exception to the rule that says life is for the living and all that." For the first time, he sounded truly angry.

"Sorry," Chris said again. "I'm laying this whole trip on you, which isn't fair and certainly isn't pleasant. I'm a real bore, aren't I?"

He didn't wait for an answer, but started off the porch without a glance back. Two steps down, he stopped suddenly, his shoulders square and rigid. Below, the lights of Laguna Beach winked and shivered.

"Maybe," Chris said, his voice hollow, "maybe I'll never be able to forget."

"Some things take a while. But never? Never's a long time."

He waited a moment, as if considering. Then he said, "Anyway, I'd better go." He took another two steps down, turned back, and added, "I really enjoyed tonight. In spite of…" He raised his arm, let it fall again, helpless to make right things that had gone wrong. "The dinner, your company…you, Annie. It was special. You've got to know that. I want you to understand how it really was, okay?"

Annie nodded. She was feeling sad for both of them. She managed a smile. "For me, too. It was very special. I won't forget…."

She watched Chris until he disappeared down the walk to the street, then took their cups back into the kitchen. She told herself that she was lucky that things hadn't gone any farther. His sudden attack of conscience was a blessing. She couldn't afford to fall in love, and that was what was happening. Things would only get messed up later, when she'd have to leave for Baja. They'd both been hurt enough in life; why pour salt into wounds by beginning a story between them that wasn't going to have a happy ending?

Chapter Four

Whatever had been her misgivings the night before, fortune was with Annie the following day.

She arose early after a restless night of sleep, dressed in her jeans and T-shirt, had coffee and was out of the house by eight o'clock.

The animal hospital was already in full swing when she arrived to check on Muffin, the waiting room packed full of people with their beloved pets, some sick, some in need of only a bath. After a ten-minute wait, she was led into the back of the complex, where Muffin was housed in a large wire cage stacked upon others of the same size. A few small furry faces peered out at her, paws pressed at the metal bars.

The vet assured Annie that Muffin was mending, although still sore and a bit groggy. Annie stayed an hour so that Muffin would not think that she was being abandoned, and agreed with the doctor that the cat should remain hospitalized a while longer, just to make sure there were no complications after the surgery. In Mexico, Annie could not be guaranteed the same medical technology as in the States.

After leaving Muffin, Annie brought her other paintings to the Haverstroms.

Hal Haverstrom was not there, having had to sit in on a bank meeting that morning, but that wouldn't be a problem. Liz said that he had given her instructions to pick out whatever appealed to her.

"You have a very good husband," Annie commented, placing the oils throughout the living room, where they could be studied individually. There were seven, as well as the four she had brought the night before.

"Hal's very good to me," Liz concurred.

She purchased one of the new oils Annie had brought with her, a wintry scene from Vail painted shortly after she had arrived there, when hope had been high that the location would offer all she had been looking for and had never found in any other place.

She wasn't surprised that Liz had chosen the painting. It was one of her best. Although it was hard to let go of the work, she needed the money and was grateful when Liz wrote the check.

For a brief instant, as she stood at the door with Liz, she was tempted to mention Chris, then thought better of it. Her interest in him could be hurtful; Annie had noted the couple's proprietary emotional investment in their son-in-law. It was still too soon for them to share him with an outsider.

Instead, she said only goodbye to Liz, and by keeping Chris's name to herself, realized that the goodbyes between them had likewise taken place in the moonlight the previous night.

Good luck continued to follow her.

When she arrived at Marge's gallery at one o'clock with the Haverstroms' check in her hand, she barely had the chance to say hello, before Marge excitedly exclaimed that she was going to have an exclusive showing of Annie's work at a gallery party to be held in three weeks.

Annie stared. "But—"

"I know, I know. Mexico. But it can wait, can't it? Mexico will still be there.

"Marge, I had planned—"

"Annie...please," Marge said, her blue eyes penetrating. "Let me put it this way. An art dealer lives to be able to discover a fabulous new artist. It happens maybe once or twice in a lifetime to major gallery owners, and let's face it, I'm not anywhere near being on that level. Now I've got myself a class act here, and I want to crow about it. This isn't just a chance for you, hon—it's a big break for me, too."

"Marge, I appreciate your confidence, but I'm really not that—"

"Yes...you are that good." Marge paused. "Look, I've used flattery—but only because it was fully warranted. Now, the only other thing that's left open to me is guilt. Big, fat, ugly, manipulative guilt. But I'm not above it, Annie. You're in my debt. The house, the referral to the Haverstroms..."

"Okay, okay!" Annie capitulated with a laugh. "Three weeks."

Marge's face lit up. "Fantastic! Now, we've got so much to plan. There's going to be champagne, of course. And I'm going to have a caterer...and not chip-

and-dip stuff. This is going to be top drawer, I promise. It's crazy, but I was thinking maybe even caviar—not as elaborate as beluga, but not as humble as lumpfish, either. Also, I'm going to have to do a bio sheet on you—"

"Uh...no, Marge. Look, I want my privacy," Annie said, her pulse starting to race. "I've never felt it's important to flash around credentials. The work itself should stand on its own."

"Yes, but—"

"I feel strongly about this, Marge. I don't care about the champagne, and as far as I'm concerned, chip-and-dip will do. If I have any conditions at all, then it's this."

Something in the way she had said it must have convinced Marge not to press the issue. "Okay," Marge relented, but with reluctance. Annie also thought she looked at her curiously, as if she hadn't entirely bought the issue of privacy. "Anyway," Marge continued a bit more soberly, "I'm going to do a few photographs of your paintings and send out flyers and some printed invitations to special clients and museum directors—"

"Museum directors? Whoa..."

"Of course museums. Why not?"

"We're not getting a bit carried away here?"

"Absolutely not. You're special, Annie. And sooner or later the world's going to know about it. I'm going to be the one responsible for making it sooner, is all. Now, I want to say you're going to be here, and maybe..." She paused, looking worried. "Any objection to having a small picture of you included on the flyer? You're gorgeous, sweetie, and if that'll draw one or two extra men with fat checkbooks in to see your work with the hope of meeting you, I say, 'why not?' What do you say?''

"I say...I say I have nothing against men with fat checkbooks who want to buy my work. Oh, and speaking of money, you just earned yourself a nice commission." She turned the Haverstrom check over to Marge, who whistled. It was for $4,500. "I can afford rent now," Annie said. "I don't like to take advantage."

And so it was decided. She was to stay in Laguna Beach for the next three weeks, renting Marge's house and using her time to paint the magnificent coastline which Marge had told her was called the American Riviera.

And for the next three weeks she might also be able to see Chris Farrentino, a desire that she did not enjoy admitting to herself.

It was also a hope that went unfulfilled.

For four days Annie painted, taking her oils and easel and canvas to a location on a bluff overlooking the Pacific. Beneath the fronds of a tall leaning palm, she painted surfers, depicting them as lonely, brave, patient Zen masters of the sea, seeking harmony in the perfect ride on the perfect wave. It was going to be a good painting.

And for four days, Chris Farrentino did not reenter her life.

The day after his date with Annie Adderly, Chris began to pack away Laura's things. He felt sorrow, but no guilt as there was no connection between discarding his past and his recent desire to make love to another woman.

Anyway, his attempt at passion had failed. Miserably and humiliatingly.

Chris started with the den. It was there that he came upon Laura's Starstream albums, along with some of their music cassettes.

For a few minutes he sat in a chair and flipped through the pages, glancing at the news clippings and thinking of how the band had meant so much to Laura, to so many people—including Annie.

He recalled the other night at Hal and Liz's, when she had made an attempt to purchase the Starstream oil. There had been an obsessive note in her plea for Hal to reconsider her offer. But Hal was a master of diplomacy, and had as gracefully and gently as possible attempted to explain his position. But in the end Chris knew that Annie had not understood there really wasn't going to be any sale.

There also wasn't going to be any relationship between them. Still, Chris thought of how she had looked, of the things she had said at dinner, and of how wonderful everything had been that night between them until— Until he had blown it.

Chris rose from the chair, taking the albums into the kitchen, where he stacked them in a box, ready to move them to the garage.

For the next five days, he didn't call Hal or Liz. They would ask about Annie, or tell him about her work. In a week she'd be gone. So he would just wait out the calendar, and then he'd be safe from making a spectacle of himself again.

He kept busy, spending as much time as possible at the police department, or out in the field doing followups on the two murders, which he was trying to link in some way. During the evenings he went to Jeff's house and went over the cases and argued until they were both hoarse. On two nights he even stayed over, falling asleep on the living room sofa.

It was on the evening of the sixth day that he found himself hot and sweaty and obsessed with the idea of seeing Annie Adderly one more time before she disappeared from his life.

As if in a trance, he drove himself to her house.

He knocked loudly on the side of the door, and waited. He peered into the living room, noticing that the screen door was latched by nothing more than a small hook.

Why did women do stupid things like that? he wondered. A hook could be jarred loose in the blink of an eye. Every day he picked up a newspaper and read that someone had been raped because she'd left her back door open. And Annie? She had left her *front* door open. Madness.

No sound came from inside. But the van was in front, so she had to be home. He knocked and called her name.

A sound. He pressed his nose against the screen and saw a small, dark shape move from behind the daybed. Her cat. Muffin, she had called it.

"Hi, Muffin," he said, as if to a human. The cat looked up, stared a moment as if assessing him with human intelligence, then issued a meow.

And then he heard another sound, "Muff...that you, baby?" and it was Annie, draped in a towel, her hair wrapped in another one, coming from the blurry darkness of the hall and into the front room.

For a minute he couldn't say anything.

Taking in her amazing beauty, now even more pronounced as she stood half-naked before him, brought all the sexual need of the evening they had spent together rushing through him. He could only stand there, rigid with fear that he was going to make a fool of himself by losing control and doing something, or saying something, that would render him a clown and haunt him for the rest of his life.

He would leave.

But before he could, he was discovered.

Annie stopped suddenly, alerted by the dark shape blocking the light at her door. Fear spread over her face. With a trembling hand she clutched her towel, then took a step back, as if to escape out the back through the kitchen. But her gaze returned to the floor, where the cat was sitting. She glanced again at the screen door, then down to the cat and darted forward, grabbing the animal into her arms.

All of this had taken place in less than a second, and it was only then that Chris found his voice.

"Annie...wait...it's me. Chris...it's Chris!"

She stopped again. For a moment she didn't move, then slowly turned her head, looking over her shoulder. "Chris?"

"It's me. Sorry to scare you like that. I was...well, I was in the neighborhood. Just thought I'd pop by." He groaned inwardly. *What a line, Farrentino. What a silver-tongued devil you are.*

Slowly she ventured closer to the door, holding the towel in place. They faced each other through the netting, like a criminal and a visitor, Chris thought. He also smelled perfume, or perhaps it was just soap. Whatever it was sent a second thrill exploding through his senses.

"Sorry," she said, "I didn't hear you knock. I was in the shower," she explained, still staring at him from behind the mesh.

"No kidding?"

She smiled, looking down at the towel. "Detective Farrentino, always picking up clues. Come on in," she said, and unlatched the small hook, opening the door for him to enter. "It'll just take me a minute..." She backed away, her eyes still on him.

"You shouldn't leave the door like that," Chris said, almost by rote. "It's not—" he was imagining what lay beneath the towel "—not safe," he finally finished, swallowing hard. He wished she would just get out of the room and put on some clothes.

"I know..." She sighed. "But the house was hot."

Chris almost laughed. He could tell her about heat, all right.

"What?" she asked, seeing his face change.

"Nothing...I—uh...maybe this wasn't a good time..." He slid his eyes over her barely covered body. "Maybe I should—"

"No, I'm glad you came," Annie said quickly. "I'll just go back and throw something on."

"Sure. I'll wait."

She turned and escaped down the hall. He heard the bedroom door close softly behind her and relaxed. God, he thought, cringing, what on earth had happened to his cool? He had come completely undone in her presence.

When she returned a few minutes later, she was dressed in a sarong. The print was a pattern of leaves, the colors all muted golds and rose, pale greens and a deep, but faded rust. With the hazy light filtering through the window and door, Chris was reminded of the Starstream painting that she had liked so much.

There was that same feeling surrounding her, that feeling of lightness, of timeless memory.

And he knew, looking at her, then—her hair floating free about her small, delicate face, her deep blue eyes twin pools of mystery—that he would never stop seeing her like this.

He was looking at her so hard that he didn't realize she had been talking to him.

"Excuse me?" he said, suddenly coming to.

"I said, can I get you a drink? There's iced tea and—"

"No, no thanks. I have to get back to work." And then there was a long silence. She was waiting. She would want to know why he had bothered to come by in the first place, if he had to leave right away. He took a deep breath and tried to sound casual.

"I just stopped by," he said, "because I ran across some old clippings and some tapes of Starstream a few days ago. I knew you were leaving, and thought that, well, you liked them a lot and you might like to see them. They belonged to—" He stopped. He didn't want to bring Laura's name up again.

"Laura?" Annie finished for him.

He wasn't sure if she was helping him out or if there was an ironic taunt to her voice. Perhaps it was only his imagination. "Right," he said simply, because they both knew it, anyway. "I thought you might like to come by before you left."

She didn't respond at once. Instead, she said, "I'm not leaving tomorrow as planned."

He felt his heart quicken. Would she say she was leaving now, within minutes, within the hour, or that very night? He had waited too long. He managed to sound casually interested, not alarmed, but surprised. "Oh? You'll be leaving sooner?"

"Later," Annie said. She walked over to a squat oak table. On it, he noticed that she had placed a plant, the kind you can pick up for three or four dollars at the supermarket. She turned the plant around so that the other side faced the sunlight coming in through the window. "I'm not going for three weeks," she went on, and at the disclosure, Chris couldn't help the smile that began at the corners of his mouth and spread until he was certain he must have worn a crooked grin.

"No Mexico?" He would have more time to see her. "You sounded so determined."

"Money," she said, looking a little sheepish. "That sounds terrible, doesn't it? Totally materialistic. But there it is—the horrible truth unveiled. Marge Briskin's giving me a solo gallery show. I promised to appear in person."

"Congratulations."

"Thanks. I think Marge is more excited than I am."

"She's got good reason. You're talented," Chris said. "You're a feather in her cap." He paused, then said, trying not to sound as if he were overanxious, "So about tonight..."

A shadow passed over Annie's face. She left the window and walked over to the sofa, but did not sit down. Instead she stood there with her back to him for a moment as if weighing something in her mind. Finally, she turned around. She bit her top lip and said, "Okay."

"Okay," Chris repeated. "Tonight."

Across the room they eyed each other knowingly, both understanding that the evening could not fail to touch them both, either disastrously or wondrously.

He left his address and telephone number and departed immediately before anything could get messed up.

Annie watched him from the window. He strode down the path, his slim buttocks outlined by the soft denim jeans. A tremor passed through her at the memory of his thighs, strong and urgent, pressed against her.

Chapter Five

She arrived a few minutes past seven. Chris had called and told her he was making them something for dinner. Of course she wasn't to expect much—but not to eat anything beforehand, either, just in case his concoction turned out.

The smell of spaghetti sauce wafted through the evening air as she made her way to his door. It was a pretty house, small, reminding her of New England. It even had small-leafed ivy weaving a lacy pattern against the white wood siding. There was a Japanese garden in front and a few large shrubs and trees.

Annie had to admit that the homeyness of the cottage and the sophistication of the semiformal garden did not mix stylistically; still, there was a pleasant sincerity about the setting, as if someone at some time had put their best efforts into creating a pleasing effect.

Chris was in jeans and a red polo shirt when he came to the door. "Ciao! Welcome to Farrentino Ristorante!" He reached to let her in, then, remembering his hands weren't clean, wiped them on a towel hanging from his back pocket.

"Umm . . . garlic." Annie wrinkled her nose pleasurably as she stepped into the house.

"Lots of it, I'm afraid. Maybe too much. I got carried away. A confession—I've only watched my mother make this concoction. You're my first victim, so to speak."

A breeze had picked up, catching Annie's hair and rustling the white fabric of her dress.

"You look beautiful," Chris said. "Oh-oh . . . wait right here . . . I sense a crisis brewing." And he left her by the door as he dashed inside the kitchen.

While he was gone, she moved farther into the living room, taking in her surroundings. It was a pretty place, warm and conventionally furnished with a mixture of contemporary and French country accents. There was a rather mediocre painting and one very nice one—a landscape—which Annie studied more thoroughly, approving of the brushwork, and a table with a collection of family photographs. Some were of Liz and Hal, others of people she didn't know, and a few with Chris. And, of course, there was Laura. There were three of Laura on the table, and looking about, Annie found another on the mantel of Chris and Laura together.

She bit her lip. Perhaps she had hoped for too much by coming into Chris's home this evening.

But Chris was back, brandishing a rose in his hand, and any chance to leave was cut off.

"No problem," he informed. "Crisis averted. Maybe I have a future in this, after all. But you'll be the judge soon enough."

The flower he held was a brilliant shade of hot pink. "From the back garden," he said proudly. "May I?" Not waiting for a response, he brushed away a lock of her hair and positioned the bloom behind her right ear. Standing back, he beamed, and said, "Perfect. You suit each other."

"May I see?" Annie said, laughing, the momentary doubt dashed by his gallantry.

"Please . . ." He gestured to an oval wall mirror, and followed as she crossed the room.

"It's pretty—the color's incredible," she said, staring at her reflection. He stood behind her, and their faces in the mirror looked much like a photograph of two beautiful people who belonged together. The thought must have occurred to Chris, too, for their eyes met, and he suddenly flushed and drew away, leaving her to stand alone in the oval frame.

"We can eat right away," he said, backing into the kitchen. "Unless you want to eat gluey pasta."

The dinner was good, and the conversation easy. Chris had set candles on the table, the flames all but unnoticeable during the early part of the dinner, with the light being bright outside. But during coffee, night had fallen, and now the small lights danced sensually.

Their words became less frequent, the lapses between their statements longer. The night had cast its spell.

"Would you like to go into the living room?" he asked, his voice husky now. "It's cooler."

"Yes. Yes, please." She stood, then looked guiltily down at the dirty dishes.

"Don't worry. The maid comes later," he said, noticing her concern.

She looked up, surprised. "Really?"

And he smiled. "No. But you're not going to have anything to do with this mess, so forget it."

He seated her in the living room, then went off for a few minutes. The picture on the mantel drew her eyes, and Annie again felt that she had made a mistake.

"You might get a kick out of seeing some of these pictures," Chris said, returning with a scrapbook. "There's some stuff in here that chronicles an entire age. Interesting stuff. Starstream represented the sixties as much as the Beatles."

Annie opened the book, while he put on one of the Starstream tapes. She hesitated as the clear, pure voice of a woman filled the room, flooding Annie's memory.

She bent her head over the brittle, aged pages of Laura Farrentino's scrapbook. She had known what to expect that night and had felt that she was equipped to face the past again.

Chris sat beside her, and they turned the pages together, looking at the different magazine and newspaper captions, stories of the band on their various tours.

It was going to be okay, thought Annie, beginning to relax more. Nothing here was scary—just more pictures that she had seen a hundred times over the past few years, some of them on posters in record shops or on albums or in people's houses...and, of course, in the homes of people like Laura Farrentino, who remembered and cherished the Starstream Age, as some had called it.

Several times she felt Chris's gaze drift from the book and study her, instead. When she glanced his way, he looked down. Once she did catch him, and they both smiled shyly, then looked away.

"Hey...I just remembered something." Chris stood, suddenly enlivened with his hidden purpose. "Be right back." He returned with a colored sheet from an old music magazine from years ago. The paper was yellowed with age. "Thought you'd like to see this, since you liked the painting of the bus so much."

Still standing, he handed it to her.

Annie took it, then stared for an instant. It was the bus, with Starstream painted across it in fluid, scrawling script, and posing in the foreground were all the members of the group: her mother, Michelle, Rod, her father, and the rest of the band. Their hair was worn long and they wore bandannas and love beads. There was even a garland of wildflowers around Michelle's long, flowing hair. She looked to Annie like a princess from a children's fairy tale. Smiling along with the rest of them was Corrie Bonner, with a laughing little girl on his shoulders. She had been that child—Canaan. She looked just about eight years old in the picture, and Annie suspected that the picture had to be one of the last taken of the whole group before the accident.

Such peace; such happiness. How it hurt to know what came after.

"Annie?"

Chris had covered her hand with his.

"Your hand was shaking."

She looked down at her hand as if to confirm his report. "Was it?" She sighed. Then, abruptly, she said, "Chris, I'm sorry, but I really should be going." She handed him the photograph and stood.

Chris looked at her, baffled. "Did I do something? Say something?"

"No."

"Annie, something had to have happened."

"No, *really*," she said, seeing that he doubted her answer. "It's nothing you said or did."

"Look, it's still early. I can't change your mind? We could do something else. Go out, if you'd like that."

She wanted to tell him everything; she wanted to share all her sorrow with him. But of course she couldn't. Their relationship did not merit the weight of her personal history. But at the very least she owed him a logical explanation. "It's nothing to do with you. It's me. It's my own sensitivity. The picture reminded me of something." She let it go at that.

But he didn't. "Reminded you of . . . ?"

"Honestly, it's not important."

"It seems like it was."

"Just of times long gone now. Of people and things I can't have back again."

His dark eyes were sympathetic, inviting. "For instance?"

She fought against the temptation to unburden herself. "I'm sorry. Really, I appreciate your interest, but it's nothing I can comfortably share. And even if I could, there's nothing either of us can do to change things from what they are." She smiled sadly and touched his face lightly, then started away. She reached for her purse on the table near the front entrance. On it was the collection of family photographs. She stopped for a moment, caught by the smiling face of Laura Haverstrom Farrentino.

Chris was beside her. She felt his eyes studying her and looked up. Their eyes met, and he shook his head. "Stupid . . . I can be really stupid sometimes. I'm sorry.

Of course you'd want to leave. I turned this whole evening into a documentary of the past, didn't I?''

He looked down to the group of family photos on the table. "The other night was bad enough, and now I invite you here, and I'm dragging out all of Laura's things to show you, her scrapbooks, everything..." He put down the music sheet. "And there's this memorial, this shrine here...and..." He exhaled. Running his fingers through his hair, he said, "No wonder you wanted to get out of here."

She dropped her eyes, feeling guilty that she was allowing him to assume he was to blame for her sudden change in mood. "Sometimes it isn't easy to deal with the past," she dissembled. Anyway, there was truth in her response; she spoke of herself.

"No, of course not. But I've got to. I'm not using you, if that's what you think. Of course that's what anyone would think. I bring you here, and I want to drag out all this stuff from the past...and still have a woman to make love to who has nothing to do with any of that. Wanting it both ways, the past and the present, and...oh, God—"

He stopped, realizing what he had just admitted.

Annie's gaze met his, and held.

He groaned, turning his eyes toward the ceiling. "Talk about a foot in the mouth. Annie...listen to me, please—"

"It's better that I go, Chris." She started out the door.

"No!" He took hold of her arm, but she didn't turn around. "Okay. I wanted to make love to you. I wanted to make love to you the first time I ever laid eyes on you. And that wasn't when I passed you on the sidewalk, either, when you were by the parking meter. I was in a restaurant, and I saw you then. My buddy was with me, and he told me to look at a twelve—he's got this juvenile rating scale for women. And I looked. He said he would kill me if I didn't at least just look. So, yes...I looked. And now it seems like looking has killed me. Because, Annie...because that one look brought me back from the dead. And now life hurts. Do you understand? Can you understand?" he repeated, his voice filled with anger and futility.

Annie nodded, still facing the screen door. The cool night air was a soothing balm.

"Good," Chris said calmly. "Good. Then at least we can agree on this one thing. The idea about the albums—that was just my stupid idea to get you here tonight. I went to see you because I just had to see you once more before you left. And the idea came to me then, that you'd like to see the Starstream stuff."

He paused, wondering if there was any point to continuing. He suddenly felt drained. But he had gone this far, and there would never be another opportunity to speak his piece. At the very least, he wanted her to know.

"I wanted *you*, Annie. I wanted you the other night, maybe more than I've ever desired a woman. And I'm sorry that things kind of collapsed on me." He laughed ruefully at his choice of words.

"I told you I understood. Those things happen—"

"They don't happen to me," Chris said, and knew he sounded like every other failed lover who protested his impotence as a phenomenon. "Except it did, this once." Now he touched her shoulder, stroked her neck beneath the silky fall of hair. "Stay, Annie. Let me show you how I feel...about you. It's not just lust. It's much, much more."

For a moment they both stood quietly, almost like statues. A clock's ticking could be heard somewhere behind them. Outside, a gust of wind whispered through the trees. Like the delicate laughter of fairies, wind chimes tinkled in a neighbor's yard.

Without turning, Annie said what she knew she must. "I'm leaving here in a few days—we both know that. And tonight's as good a time as any for both of us to face up to things, before things get . . . complicated."

"Why the hell did you come here, then?" he asked her.

"Why?" She hesitated, then with a slight, bitter laugh, said, "Because I wanted you, too. But it was stupid. A stupid dream that has no point."

"Why?"

"Because it will never work. So why make things more rotten for ourselves than they already are?"

"Have you ever considered that there's no reason that they couldn't work out? I'm not saying that they will, or that they have to. All I'm suggesting, Annie, is that there is that possibility. *If* you'd just give it a chance—give us a chance. You don't have to go to Mexico."

She gave him a stricken look, as if he had slapped her. "You can't know what I must or mustn't do. You don't know the first thing about me."

She slipped from him then, disappearing into the night, as, bewildered, he watched her from the door. For a while he stood there, expecting to hear the sound of a motor start up and to see the arc of lights pass over the shrubbery as she drove off. His expectation was met with nothing but still darkness.

Suddenly concerned, he stepped outside and quickly traced Annie's steps down to the street. He was at a full run, scenes of front-page mayhem practically blinding him, when he saw her. She was returning up the walk to his house.

Seeing him, she stopped. For a moment, flooded with relief, so did he. Then, at a slower pace, he continued the rest of the way until they again faced each other.

Both seemed at a loss as to what to say. When a long moment had passed, her voice sounded in the darkness.

"I couldn't go," she said sheepishly.

It was all she needed to say. Chris picked her up and, carrying her like a new bride, took her into the house again, this time to the bedroom.

The four-poster bed made a sound like a soft sigh when their bodies came together. Chris was over her, entwining his hands with both of hers over her head. "Are you sure?" he said.

Annie nodded. "Completely." The light from the hallway spilled across them, softening the lines of their bodies, casting a glow over their faces. "Are *you*?" she whispered back, searching his face with her dark blue eyes.

"Oh, yes . . ." Chris murmured. "Oh, yes, I'm very, very sure."

And he lowered himself over her, moving his mouth hungrily from her lips, downward, to the indentation of her neck, to her collarbone and lower to her breasts. At the pleasure, Annie stiffened, taking in a sharp breath, and arched against him. Chris trembled, staying himself for a moment. "Not yet . . . not yet . . ." he whispered, cautioning himself to make the pleasure endure.

His tongue was velvet soft on her abdomen. He continued to run his hands over her body, exploring the fullness of her breasts, the sweep of her silken hips. His breathing was rapid, growing urgent and ragged as he buried his face lower.

Behind Annie's closed lids came bursts of brilliant light, explosions matching the spasms beginning in her groin and radiating outward until it felt that her body was dissolving in a sea of blissful sensation.

Chris's back was hot and slippery as she pressed her fingers against his smooth, hard muscles, which rippled with his every movement. He was calling her name, and all she could do was respond with the pressure of her fingers, words that she might have answered lost to the delirious sensations he was causing.

But he understood her soundless responses, and kissing her again, he raised himself and held her face between both his hands. "Now..."

"Yes," she said, and slowly, he dropped his body atop hers, their skin hot and wet, and then proceeded with the beginning...the true beginning.

With one hand, he parted her legs, sliding effortlessly into her heat, not at once, but with a movement that seemed to last an eternity. Their lips were joined, and he discovered the feel of her, all of her. They held still then, and finally, with a thrust and a cry they were joined completely.

Annie opened her eyes, seeing the high cheekbones, the shadow of his beard, the sweep of thick lashes over the dark eyes, which he now opened slowly.

"Annie...oh...my love, Annie..." And then he closed his eyes once again.

He moved slowly, as if to a soundless refrain, lost in its beat. And, she, too, was caught up in the web of bewitchment, her body undulating to the driving force of Chris's movements.

They cried out together, the moment building, coming upon them with the force of a whirlwind, and then, blinding passion.

Dimly, from far away, she heard her voice call his name, a response from Chris . . . and they were coming together again, then parting, joining, their bodies caught in an electrical storm of arcing desire.

The spell, the storm, the wild abandonment ebbed, and in time there was another softer and more luxuriant period of soft coupling, their bodies moving in a gentle, languorous way that led them eventually into the cradle of deep sleep.

Chapter Six

Upon waking, the first sound Chris heard was a blue jay chirping outside the bedroom window. His eyes slowly adjusted to the brightness.

There was a woman in his arms...a beautiful, warm, magnificently desirable woman. For an instant his lids fell closed again, as if he was afraid that he would awaken from the dream. But Annie sighed, shifting against him, her fingers resting near a tangle of brown-gold hair.

She was real. Last night had happened.

And for Chris, it was almost too impossibly good to believe.

As if she had heard his thoughts, Annie began to stir again, her dark brown lashes fluttering open in fits and starts, until, wide-eyed, she stared back at him.

"Morning," he whispered, almost unable to contain the happiness. He wanted to snatch her up into his arms, to lift her high into the air and toss her like a small child. He could go on catching her forever.

She said nothing for a moment, merely continued looking. "Chris..." she said driftily, her voice still faint with sleep. She stretched slightly beneath the covers. "Morning..."

They exchanged shy smiles, memories of the night's sensual abandonment a bit too intense for the daylight.

"Sleep okay?"

She nodded, looking about her. "A four-poster..." she said, almost wondrously. "I've never slept in a four-poster bed. It was something I always wanted."

To Chris, she appeared the most beautiful, most adorable creature that God had ever created. "You look perfect in one."

"I feel perfect in it," she said, and reached to pull him to her.

But the telephone put a stop to a morning's encore of the night before, its shrill voice summoning Chris to the nightstand.

Sitting with his back propped against two pillows, he spoke for a moment about something having to do with work, idly tracing Annie's bare collarbone with his slender fingers. She, in turn, crooked her neck and managed to kiss the back of his hand, then slid from the covers and straddled his waist.

His conversation faltered.

She laughed mischievously and continued to torment him.

Chris placed his hand over the phone's mouthpiece in an attempt to mute their laughter. But it was almost impossible to carry on an intelligent conversation with the feel of her bare breasts rubbing provocatively against his chest, her lips kissing his eyes, his ears, her hands running along his arms.

The call was finally terminated, and Chris grabbed her, laughing, and with a pagan yell threw her backward onto the bed, raised himself over her and growled menacingly, "So you'll toy with me, will you? A dangerous enterprise, my pretty." Silencing her squeals and giggles, he easily slid his body over hers. "I can't say you're hard to overpower."

"I'm always attacking men like this—it's exhausting business."

Chris laughed.

And so did she, along with nipping at his neck. "It makes me hungry!"

"Ow!" he said. "You *are* trouble after all, aren't you?" He was playing, they were playing, they were making a different kind of love, and it was light and happy and therefore totally unexpected when the picture on the dresser passed across Chris's vision as he tussled with his willing victim.

Laura. Her smile in the photograph cut off his breath. And the eyes...the trusting eyes mocked his joy as being stolen pleasure.

Annie saw the change sweep over his face, even before he slowly removed himself physically from their embrace. It was as if another man had suddenly taken possession of his soul.

"I'd better go," he said with a quick, perfunctory kiss. "Duty calls...."

He didn't even look at her, instead averting his eyes to a distant, unseen object. And then he was gone, showering in the bathroom with the door between the two rooms closed.

Changing her position on the bed, she looked around, seeing the room from Chris's perspective, and easily discovered the cause of Chris's sudden change of mood.

Of course, she thought. But of course. And she closed her eyes, imagining what he must have experienced when he looked at the sweet, happy face of his wife. Last night had been his first time with another woman.

Annie opened her eyes again and stared across at the picture on the dresser, the eyes of Laura Farrentino now holding hers. But Annie did not feel rebuke in their gaze. She saw understanding. And in her heart, she felt the other woman's kind, accepting presence.

Her conversation with Chris was cordial but stilted while he dressed for work. He seemed embarrassed, but there was nothing Annie could do to help him. There was some vague talk from him about catching up with her later. And then he was gone, leaving her instructions on how to turn the inside lock on the front door when she left.

The truth was, she harbored a certain degree of secret shame on her own account. She had a past of her own to face, one that she had run from her entire life. And now, if she wanted to remain in Chris Farrentino's life, she would have no other choice but to confront her own shadowy demons.

Either that or one day soon she would be headed down another highway, the proverbial rolling stone that gathers no moss . . . and knows no love.

She was almost home when the Volkswagen's wheel started acting up. At first she thought it was a flat, because the tire wobbled. But then a howling sound started, and she knew it was something else, something more serious and therefore more expensive.

Woefully, she analyzed her situation. She doubted she could make it all the way down the hill to a repair shop. On the other hand, there wasn't far to go until she reached home. Taking a gamble that the wheel's ailment would hold out until then, she held her breath and continued up the hill, inching her way along.

The vibration worsened; the howl became a grating yowl, and it felt as if her rear left wheel had locked and was being dragged up the hill by the efforts of the other three. It didn't feel as if anything was wrong with the brakes, but what if...?

A terrible, macabre thought passed through her mind as she wobbled perilously toward her destination: what irony if Chris lost both his women. But it was a cruel thought, and she rejected it immediately, feeling awful that she had even thought it.

He feared the worst when he arrived at her house at a little past four in the afternoon. During the morning, he had kept himself occupied with police business, but even then, thoughts of Annie kept intruding.

He knew he had behaved badly that morning. His sudden change of mood must have seemed totally incomprehensible to her. And she was so sensitive, too. It seemed hard enough for her to trust without having to deal with his rejection in the morning.

He parked his car, then took the incline from the street up to her house, his head lowered as he walked with his hands thrust deep within the pockets of his slacks. He was thinking of what he would say. He had dressed more formally that day, having had some official meetings, and wore a lightweight jacket over an oxford shirt, now minus the tie.

When he reached the porch, he took the first two steps before noticing that he was being watched by four sets of eyes—two blue human ones, and two yellow, the latter belonging to a gray-and-white cat.

"Hi," Annie said when he stopped short and stood looking up at her. Her tone was noncommittal. She peered at him from an angle, leaning past the easel. A paintbrush was in one hand.

"Hi," he said back, wishing he knew where he stood with her. "How goes it?" It was an absurdly light opening, given the weight of his thoughts, but he didn't know how else to begin.

"You don't really want to know," Annie said, and dipped her brush into a glob of vermilion paint on a wooden pallet.

So, Chris thought miserably, she *had* taken offense at his behavior. "Listen, about what happened this morning... I need to explain—"

"Not really." Her voice came from behind the canvas.

He wished he could see her face. "No, I do—I want to. What happened had to do with me... not with *us*," he said, and was immediately pleased that he had managed to put it so well. The explanation was clean and concise and, best of all, true.

"I know," said Annie.

But her voice, even though she claimed to understand, did not, in fact, sound forgiving.

"Annie!" His voice rang in the afternoon stillness. "You think you might come out from behind that wall? I'd like to talk to you, not a blank—"

"Listen," she cut in, still invisible, "I've got my own problems. And one of them is making enough money to pay for all the things in my life that are apparently falling apart—such as my cat and now my car. So, if you don't mind, just say what you have to say—which I already told you isn't really necessary—and leave me alone to earn a living. Okay?"

"What?"

"I said—"

"No, I heard what you said. What I mean is what happened to your car?"

"Something with the wheel. It's...I don't know...it makes a terrible noise and it wobbles, and now it hardly goes at all."

"Sounds like a frozen bearing."

"I don't know the technical problem, but I can tell you the poor old thing's totally out of sorts."

"Ah," Chris said. "I get it. You're identifying—now you're all out of sorts, too."

Annie's brush stopped moving. He heard her laugh. And then she put her brush down and was at long last coming into view from behind the canvas.

"Sorry," she said contritely. Her blue eyes sparkled in the afternoon light, reminding Chris of fire opals. "I guess it's my time to apologize for being...difficult. It had nothing to do with you. I got crabby because of the car." She sighed and lifted the back of her hair off her neck. "It just seems like one thing after the next lately. I set off for Mexico, and my cat got sick—one major expense, let me tell you. And then I have this new thing with the wheel—and you know how these places take you, especially if you're a woman alone."

"But you aren't," Chris said, impulsively stepping forward and taking her in his arms. "You aren't alone."

She looked up at him and shook her head slightly. "Oh, Chris, last night was wonderful, but it was...let's face it—it was what it was."

"And what was that?" he asked, his eyes serious.

Annie looked away, but did not pull from his embrace. "Two people who like each other, who are attracted to each other, who needed each other...being together for one night."

"Oh. Is that what it was for you? I wanted more than a night, Annie."

"A week of nights, then. But in three weeks, Chris—"

"What's wrong with you?" he asked. The way he said it might have been construed as being in jest. But he repeated the question a second time, and clearly he was asking for a serious response. "I don't get it, Annie. You have this thing about leaving here—this three-week thing—and on the other hand you have this totally unstructured lifestyle. At least that's the impression you give. So what's the story?"

This time she did pull away, but Chris pulled her back.

"Tell me," he said in a tone that sounded more demanding than he had wished.

In response, Annie glared at him. She yanked her arm free of his hold and, stepping back a few paces, said, "There's nothing so mysterious about it. I made myself a promise that I'd be in Mexico...that I'd be there and I'd paint, and I—"

"And I don't buy any of this," he said flatly.

They faced each other like two bitter adversaries. Then Chris relented, softening his stance. "Look, I'm not going to play any games. You mean something to me. Call last night a mutual exchange of needs if you want to. But for me it was something else. Something more. And I want to hold on to you. What you're telling me just doesn't grab me as being totally up front. That's why I'm pressing you. I can't help it. It's my nature. If something doesn't make sense, I go looking for the reasons why. Maybe that's why I'm in the detective business."

Annie turned away, understanding him perfectly, and knowing that she was the worst kind of coward for not telling him the whole story. Because, sooner or later, not knowing the truth was going to hurt him, just as it had others who had cared about her.

Maybe, she thought, if he were just a guy, any other guy—some real-estate entrepreneur or a restaurant manager—anything but a cop, she could tell him. But Chris wouldn't let things rest once he knew the facts. No, being Chris, he would want to open up the past again. He would want to track down Corrie Bonner to make sure she could be safe. It sounded sensible and logical, but reality didn't always work the way people supposed it would. Corrie had escaped and no one had been able to find him years ago, when the case was a major story. What could Chris do now, but dredge up a lot of unpleasant memories and make her life hell again?

It was Chris who finally let her off the hook, relenting, offering her a tour of the surrounding area. "Places the ordinary tourist doesn't see—but an artist must."

Before they set off, he also addressed the matter of the Volkswagen wheel. Marge had instructed the phone company to turn the phone back on, and there was a friendly hum when Chris picked up the receiver to call a friend of his who worked on the police vehicles. They were one of the few departments that had an on-site repair shop.

"He said he'll take a look at it when he's off work," Chris informed Annie.

"How much—"

"Don't worry about the cost—he owes me a favor or two."

The ride improved Annie's mood considerably, and Chris was right: she did get to see the hidden Laguna Beach, the secret places off the beaten track of the ordinary tourist.

Her eyes drank in the rich beauty of the inland valley. High outcroppings of rock showed evidence of having once been submerged beneath the sea, which had receded over the millennia to form the present coastline. There were deep crevices and caves in the red, pitted face of rock, where the petrified forms of primeval crustaceans clung, along with the tenacious roots of living plants.

And on the valley floor, there were long expanses of rolling green terrain dotted with the gnarled and spreading branches of ancient trees. Barbed-wire fences kept grazing cattle from wandering into danger.

The coastline and valleys for miles inland had once been a Spanish land grant, Chris said, belonging to one family. In-fighting among relatives had subsequently been responsible for the ranch's division into smaller parcels. Over the years much of the land had fallen into multiple private ownership. Now, the land grabbers representing giant development corporations were in a frenzy to once again gather the individual plots into huge undivided acreage.

"This is one of the most expensive tracts of land in the United States," he said. "The developers would like to turn everything into concrete. It won't be long before this place is filled with driveways and BMWs."

"It seems a crime," Annie said.

"So far it has been. The state's had a moratorium on using the land for commercial development for years. But money always wins out, and eventually some guy with enough cash to influence the decision makers is going to build his tract homes."

"I'd love to paint here," Annie said wistfully. "To show it as it is now."

"Then you'd better paint fast," Chris said. "Because these trees won't be here for long. There'll be bulldozers, instead."

Their tour lasted three hours, and when they arrived back at Annie's cottage, the wheel on the van had been repaired.

Annie was elated. "I can't believe it!" she said, watching as Chris stooped down and checked out the work. "How could he fix it so fast? I mean, wouldn't he have had to drive it somewhere? And I've got the key."

"Probably hot-wired it," Chris guessed, standing.

"But that's illegal."

Chris smiled. "You know what they say—we guys on the side of the law are just the flip side of the bad guys. Same minds working different sides of the street. Both tricky."

"I'll remember that," she said, and laughed. "Anyway, I really appreciate it." They walked together up the hill to the house. "I'd like to thank him. Maybe take him out for lunch or something?"

"I'm sure a simple phone call would suffice."

"Okay. How about now?"

Chris dialed his friend's number, while Annie waited for him to hand her the receiver.

"Gus? Chris. You did a great job, pal." A pause. "The van." A longer pause. "Oh. No, that's the address." Chris looked at Annie, then turned his face from her view and said with a note of concern, "Hey...are you being straight about this?" He waited, said, "Thanks—catch you later." Then slowly he put the receiver down.

"What?" Annie said.

Chris looked at her. "Gus didn't fix it."

Annie stared. "What?"

"He said he didn't fix it. He came by, but the van wasn't here. He thought maybe he had the wrong place, but he repeated the address to me and it was okay—Gus had it right."

For a moment they stared at each other. Then Annie's gaze began to waver and finally she turned away, making a shaky start into the kitchen. "Iced tea?" Her voice quavered slightly.

Chris didn't say anything. Instead, he followed her, and as she swung open the refrigerator door, he pressed it closed. Taking her gently by the shoulders, he turned her around. He lifted her chin. "What's going on here, Annie?"

She hesitated. "I thought maybe some iced tea—"

"Forget the iced tea. I want to know what's going on here?" Chris repeated darkly.

Annie felt trapped. Nothing would make any sense now but to tell him the truth. She would have to tell him that she was afraid, really afraid. It was happening again—the strange favors, the unseen, unknown helping hand. But if she told him the truth, then he would start looking into the dark corners of her life. She couldn't risk that.

"I don't know," Annie said. "Maybe a neighbor came by."

"What neighbor?"

"I don't know *what* neighbor. How would I know that? I was with you. I came back here and the wheel was fixed, and how am I to know—"

"You don't make sense," Chris said angrily.

"Well, I'm sorry," she said defiantly. "I'm sorry I don't have all the answers all the time."

"What are you afraid of?" he persisted, not letting her sidetrack him into a petty argument.

"Of you!" she shot back. "I'm afraid of having a man I hardly know suddenly think he can move into my life and control every part of it. Sleeping together once doesn't exactly give anyone access to a person's private life."

Chris didn't say anything. By his expression she might just as well have dashed a bucket of frigid water in his face. Then, as the silence persisted, he slowly recovered and said, "Sorry," and turned.

Annie watched as he walked through the living room, and straight out the front door, not looking back.

Chris was consumed with a profound sense of loss as he made his way down the front path. How could Annie have taken something so precious between them and chalked it all up to lust? Unless she was denying... unless...

Who did fix the wheel?

Finally as he sat looking out the windshield of his Honda Prelude, he gave into a spasm of jealousy. She was involved with someone else. That had to be it. What else could possibly account for her car suddenly having been fixed?

Maybe she was running from the guy. The guy was hounding her, but she wasn't really interested in keeping him out of her life. Chris knew such games went on between men and women, although he couldn't imagine how a person's mind could get so warped.

Now two sets of emotions vied for supremacy in him: jealousy on one hand, protectiveness on the other.

To say he was confused and tortured was not to do his situation justice as he drove past the green Volkswagen van with its mysteriously mended wheel.

Chapter Seven

It had finally happened, thought Annie. After years of running, she was trapped.

If it had been any other time, she would be shooting down the highway in her green van without looking back, fleeing from her unseen, unwanted benefactor. Instead, all Annie could do was move about the cottage, busying herself with odds and ends. Occasionally, she would stop and stare into space as she considered her position and searched in vain for alternatives.

She watered the plants sitting on the railing of the back stoop. How had he found her?

In the bathroom she refolded towels that were already neatly arranged. How did he always know what she needed?

She scoured the clean kitchen sink. And why did he always help her?

Standing at the front window, she looked out, pondering. What did he want from her?

The questions haunted her.

Exhausted from the mental turmoil, she turned from the window and sank slowly into the soft comfort of a frayed armchair. She must not panic; she must consider her options. There had to be a solution. There *had* to be.

Over the years there had been a string of incidents similar to the wheel's mysterious repair, all unexplainable. Before the wheel, there had been Muffin's red collar. Before that, door locks had been fixed, a window repaired, even a hospital bill paid when she had broken her leg. Although each gesture had been an obvious act of kindness, there was a creepy quality to having a phantom godfather...or godmother, for all she knew.

A few times she had thought to talk to the police, but supposed that they would only think she was some paranoid crackpot out to get attention.

In fact, once, years ago, she had called the police. She had spoken to the desk sergeant on duty, speaking anonymously about her plight. In the middle of the conversation she had hung up, realizing from his flip and aggravated response that he thought she was nothing more than a wigged-out crank. She didn't blame him.

When people were being mugged on the streets, Annie could see how the police wouldn't be unduly concerned about a woman complaining that someone kept looking out for her best interests.

Now she couldn't go anyplace; Muffin simply was not well enough. And there was also the gallery show that she had committed herself to attending. Flyers announcing her personal appearance at the party, along with her picture on it, were already being printed by Marge at considerable expense. And of course, Annie needed the money from a few sales.

Then there was Chris.

For the first time in her life, she did not want to say goodbye to a man.

It could mean trouble. Only once before had she seriously tried to stay in one place. Even now, years later, she could feel the panic. Her secret had been discovered by a news reporter.

Canaan Palance, Starstream's Lost Child. The lost daughter of two of the most romantic and legendary performers in American musical history, has surfaced in Coral Gables, Florida, under the pseudonym of Annie Adderly.

That was to have been the reporter's big story. The only reason it had never been broken to the press, Annie found out later, was that he had been reassigned to Central America, where he got caught up in a lot of bang-bang reporting. His newfound status as a political reporter must have eclipsed his appetite for show biz sensationalism.

But what he had found out about her life was true.

Michelle and Rod Palance, founders and lead singers of Starstream, had been her parents. Along with the rest of the group, they had perished in the crash of the Starstream bus just before dawn one misty morning. It had been a tragic end of a group that had already been mythologized by an adoring public, and their fate only served to solidify their legendary status.

The only survivors were Canaan, and the man who had engineered the accident—Corrie Bonner, the group's ex-drummer.

And from that terrible morning on, Canaan Palance had never felt safe.

She had been eight years old when the accident had occurred. The night before the band had pulled out for San Francisco, she had been dropped off by her mother in Bakersfield, California. Her mother's friend, a singer she had toured with before Starstream, was to watch over her until her mother, Michelle, came back; that was to have been soon—in one, maybe two days.

That had never happened. Instead, there was the tragedy.

There were no close relatives on either side of Annie's family. That was one of the reasons the Starstream group had become so tightly knit—both Michelle and Rod had made the members of the band their family. Her mother's friend had wanted to keep her after the accident, but the social welfare agency had denied the petition for guardianship. Years before, the woman had been arrested for taking contraband across the Canadian border—the contraband being a euphemism for drugs. Although the woman swore that she had been clean for years, the home Michelle's friend offered was perceived as an inappropriate environment for a child.

Instead, Canaan was sent to live with foster families after the accident, her name changed to Annie to protect her from fans and members of the media, who, in their fascination over Starstream, would have made her life into a sideshow.

And there was Corrie Bonner, Starstream's drummer, though technically Corrie had no longer been a member of the band.

The night before the accident, he had parted ways with the group when Rod Palance, Annie's father, had fired him during a fight over Michelle. The scene, witnessed by several people in the motel parking lot, had been violent, with threats made by both men to exact future vengeance on the other.

Because Corrie had been the group's unofficial mechanic, it was a foregone conclusion that Corrie had rigged the accident by tampering with the bus's steering column.

An arrest warrant had been issued but was never served. Corrie had disappeared.

Yet speculation persisted that a man unbalanced enough to commit a crime as heinous as that against Starstream would not rest easy until he had accomplished the entire vendetta by finishing off Canaan, too.

The fear of Bonner, therefore, had become the second reason that Canaan became Annie Adderly, dropping the Palance and using Adderly.

At seventeen, finished with high school, Annie left her last foster home. Working full-time, she attended junior colleges where tuition had been within her means. The money made by the group had been poorly managed. Annie's parents were artists, not business people, and although now and then a small pile of money accumulated for Annie in royalty checks, which were deposited in a San Francisco account under her name, most of the group's financial proceeds were eaten away by administrative costs. The bulk of Starstream's royalties had been assigned to other individuals—personal managers, agents, publicists, attorneys—for proffessional favors the group had obtained years ago when they were green and idealistic. Blissfully naive of material concerns, they had lived the idealistic life conveyed in their songs.

Annie studied drawing and painting, finding an outlet in creative expression for her buried emotions. Her talent was as radiantly obvious as her beauty, both attracting admirers.

Her art, if not her personal life, flourished. Her work sold in galleries and in sidewalk art shows. Private collectors approached her for commissioned work. Still, the rhythm of her life drew her onward down other highways. Eventually she ended up in Florida.

There she met a retired air force colonel, who took great interest in her artwork. He was an older man, seasoned with wisdom. Acting solely as a good friend to her, perhaps even as a surrogate father, he gave her the strength she needed to remember the joyous days of her early childhood.

It was during this period when she painted Starstream, the oil hanging in Hal Haverstrom's living room.

She had painted the bus as a distant memory, its image fuzzy, muted, as if seen through tears. The painting's power, commented on by all who saw the canvas, came from its very softness and the impression of innocence, which was, after all, the essence of the Starstream legend.

And so, in the completion of the painting, Annie experienced the elation of freedom. Her art had allowed her to safely return to the past. She had confronted the feelings of loss, and therefore could move on in her life, which paradoxically meant not going anywhere at all.

For an entire year, she had lived in peace. She had a small apartment of her own and had developed a number of friends.

And then came the surprise party the colonel threw for her birthday. What was to have been a happy occasion became her undoing.

One of the couples invited asked to bring a friend. The friend was a journalist, an insightful and charming man, who, seeing the Starstream oil on the wall, became immediately intrigued. He had questions.

The painter's name was Canaan?

Yet didn't Annie paint the bus?

But...

And then he pieced together the puzzle, recalling that the little girl who survived the Starstream disaster was called Canaan.

Annie panicked as he questioned her about Starstream's last night, proposed that she allow him to interview her for an article on Starstream....

No, not just an article, a whole book.... And why not? So many people loved the group. Part of the Beatles era.

Everyone waited expectantly for her to agree, for her to tell them all about what it had been like, what had happened between Annie's mother and her father and the murderer, Corrie Bonner.

The following day Annie slipped out of town.

In the next big city she sold the Starstream painting to a gallery. The gesture was a peace offering to the demon that still haunted her.

There was no doubt in her mind that if she were to tell Chris about the phantom benefactor, he would do everything in his power to help her unearth the mystery. But in solving the one problem, he would undoubtedly stumble on her true identity. If her identity became known publicly, she would be at the continuous mercy of the press and Starstream's die-hard fans.

They would poke, they would pry, they would make her repeat again and again the sorrowful story of that fateful night.

And then there was the threat of Corrie Bonner. Any publicity could draw him to her. She could imagine the headlines then!

Shivering, she rose to her feet and looked about. Then, without a second thought, she grabbed her portable easel, her box of paints and a fresh canvas and headed out the door.

A half-hour later, she was tracing her way back to the virgin land where Chris had taken her. How happy she had been then. The feeling would come again, she hoped, just from being there. She drove with the windows down. The sunlight was warm, the ocean breeze refreshing.

She parked the van at a shallow ravine just off the blacktop, to shield it from notice of possible vandals and further avoid being apprehended by the police for trespassing. Off to the side there was a dirt road leading into the valley. It would have made a more convenient entrance, but it was marked Private and she didn't want to court an irate property owner's wrath. So she left her van obscured by a stand of bushy oleander shrubs waving gently in white and pink bloom and dragged out her artist's tools.

It wasn't easy to lug her paraphernalia across the fields and up a hill, negotiating her way around large groupings of rocks, but eventually she made it to an ideal location. Somehow she had lost her bearings. It wasn't the same place Chris had shown her, but it was every bit as pleasing to the senses.

The knoll overlooked a magnificent rock formation, tropical vegetation sprouting from its deep fissures. Juxtaposed against the natural splendor was a small white ranch house, its lawn consisting of native grasses and stalky wildflowers. Its driveway was dirt mixed with particles of pea gravel. Some construction was going on, by the looks of some scaffolding assembled along one side of the house. There were also stacks of wood roofing shingles, partly covered by a tarp. One end was loose and flapped in the breeze.

She set up her easel and sat on the small portable stool she used for such on-site occasions. Within a half-hour, all her troubles were distant memories, her mind engrossed in the images taking form on her canvas. Her hand moved as if by itself.

The house looked as if it were emerging from a dream—it shimmered with white-gold light, its undistinguished form taking on an emotional grandeur that blended with the softness of the surrounding natural environment.

And then, suddenly, unexpectedly the picture changed.

Annie stilled, jarred from her reverie as a door slammed shut and a man appeared.

With his head bent, he whistled a random tune and moved toward the car parked in the dirt driveway. A moment later a second man emerged from the house, this time leaving the door open behind him as he shouted something to the first. Annie couldn't make out what was said. The first man looked up from where he stood by the car's open door.

At the sight of his face Annie froze. *It was Corrie Bonner.*

She closed her eyes. *No*, she told herself. *No.*

Her heart pounded like a jackhammer. All the warnings of the police and social welfare workers and the executor of her parents' estate came back to her. Corrie Bonner was evil or crazy or both. She hadn't remembered Corrie like that, but they said she'd been a child at the time and didn't understand. Corrie was a murderer, they said. And there was no guarantee that he wouldn't try to find her and kill her, too.

And now he was within shouting distance.

She looked again, and the man she thought she had recognized as Corrie Bonner was in the car, almost hidden from view. The second man stood waving from the driveway, a smile on his face.

Her hands shook as she threw her paints and brushes in her metal case, put away her pallet and folded her easel. The small collapsible chair seemed impossibly awkward to handle.

The car started up, pulled leisurely from the driveway, then edged slowly onto the dirt road.

Annie saw the second man turn and walk back into the house. The door closed.

It was quiet again, so quiet that she could almost hear the blood flowing through her veins.

Her thoughts were scrambled and it was hard to walk. Her lungs filled with dry, heated air. She felt as if she were breathing in solid dust. Her temples pounded. She wanted to hide, to run from the nightmare, but it wasn't a dream. Everything seemed brighter, sharper. The reality made her heart race as she struggled through the high grasses.

She had almost reached her van when to the right she heard a car turn into the dirt road below the hill. A dark blue car appeared, a small compact Ford, dust trailing behind it. She watched for a moment behind some bushes as it made its way toward the white ranch house. In another instant it was gone.

And she was safe.

She had reached her Volkswagen bus parked off the side of the road behind the stand of high oleander shrubs and was just closing its side door when the dark blue Ford returned, this time moving at high speed. As it reached the blacktop, it flashed past Annie, a blur of dark blue metal, a rental car sticker on the bumper— Dart-Away Rentals. The man at the wheel wore a cap, blue and yellow, his shadowed profile hard and grim beneath the visor.

Then, just for an instant, as if sensing an observer, he turned his head. Were it not for the shrubbery, they would have been face-to-face. Even so, the high branches, heavy with flowers, parted in a passing breeze, and then, in that fraction of an instant, she saw him. The sunlight played harshly over his features, blanching the angles and contours. Only the eyes remained in bold relief. Wary, dark beacons, they scanned the landscape. Had he seen her?

He lost control of the vehicle.

The car fishtailed once, was brought back to its course and sped away, going in the direction of the freeway.

Peace returned.

On the other side of the road, some cows had ambled to the fence. Patiently, they chewed the summer's grass. A hawk circled above, looping gracefully in the air as it looked for prey.

At any other time, Annie might have found the scene beautiful, but now she did not like being watched, even by some dumb and innocent beasts; and when the hawk swooped quickly down, she remembered that he was not only graceful, he was a killer.

Chapter Eight

Chris sat in his office. He had a slight headache. Pressing his knuckles against a pressure point on the side of his temple, he tried to concentrate on his job.

Around him the buzz of cops' voices mingled with the beeping of electronic equipment, retorts by female staffers and the racket of a printer. Someone nearby was having an argument with someone else on the telephone.

But Chris hardly heard any of this. It was all just white noise as he stared at his computer screen on which various dates and sentences were underlined. Clues. Clues that made no sense. Clues that were clues, but led nowhere in the two murders he was trying to link together.

Chris tried harder to focus, to make some sense out of the nonsensical. He even narrowed his eyes, struggling to see something that he kept overlooking. A dull sinus ache throbbed behind his forehead.

It was no use. His mind wasn't really on crime. In actuality, the computer screen was little more than a humming electronic blur before him.

He thought of other things, dwelling on the greatest mystery of all time—women...that strange, incomprehensible, baffling, annoying, difficult opposite sex. And Annie Adderly personified her gender perfectly. *She* was giving him the headache, not the barometric pressure or pollen or job stress.

He would never give her up.

Having thought it, Chris brought his fist down from his temple and let his hand thump emphatically on the desktop.

Current headache aside, since meeting Annie, he had felt good. He felt like a man again. His adrenaline pumped in all the right places, at all the right times. His libido was ticking away, at the ready to rise to the proper occasion—so to speak.

Chris sank back into his chair, and rocked back and forth on its springs, thinking hard.

A dinner invitation would be refused outright. He knew that without even having to think twice.

If he just dropped by again, she'd give him the cold shoulder, unless he had some major reason for appearing on her doorstep.

What did she want? Or need? And then it came to him. *The Starstream painting.* That was it: the painting of the bus. He nodded to himself, staring at the monitor as if the screen contained the future. He would entice her to dinner at Hal and Liz's by suggesting that she speak to Hal again about the chance of purchasing the oil. Of course, Chris went on to consider, he would not be dishonest; there would have to be a basis in reality for this plan or he would be dangling a stick without a carrot.

During lunchtime he dropped by Hal's office in South Laguna. Like his home, Hal's office was set up in the hills, with a view of the ocean. It was a three-story concrete-and-glass structure. Hal owned the entire building, most of which housed Haverstrom Corporation's own facilities, with a small portion of the complex leased to an escrow company and a commodities' brokerage firm. In the center of the complex was a spectacular atrium, the top closed in by a translucent skylight, beneath which grew full-sized ficus trees surrounding a Japanese reflecting pond stocked with large koi fish.

Hal was pleased to see him, welcoming him as if he were royalty. Without being asked, Hal's secretary delivered a tray with coffee and small triangular sandwiches—cucumber, chicken, and ham. The serving pieces were sterling silver and bone china.

"You may not like my reason for coming," Chris said, taking his place in one of the four chairs opposite Hal's imposing rosewood desk. The office was furnished with expensive modern furniture. Several important paintings hung throughout the room—a Neiman skier, a limited edition Chagall lithograph, an original Earle and an early Warhol of Marilyn Monroe.

At Chris's declaration, Hal arched his brows. His voice sounded pleasant, slightly amused. "Oh?"

"I've been seeing Annie Adderly."

Hal's eyes flickered briefly. Then the brilliant blue gaze stabilized, serene again as he stared at Chris from across the desk.

Hal had always intrigued Chris. His father-in-law had the gift of the consummate poker player—the ability to hide all emotion.

"And you've come to ask for my blessing," Hal said.

Chris hesitated. He didn't exactly like to think of it that way, but in some ways it was true. Over the past seven years, Hal and he had become like father and son. But like any relationship between two men, especially father and son, to be a complete male meant standing alone, being true to one's own self.

Chris seized the challenge. "Of course, I'd like it if you were happy... or, at least, understanding."

"But, regardless, you are going to start living your own life."

Hal Haverstrom did not ask questions. At the very least, he stated, and more generally he dictated to others. That he exercised his sense of control with charm only increased his effectiveness. On many occasions Hal had tried to manipulate Chris into following some course of action. His methods had been so subtly engineered that Chris had almost succumbed to Hal's wily machinations. In the end, however, Chris had stood his ground, choosing to act on his own judgment, and Hal had never held his sense of independence against him. In fact, Chris was under the impression that Hal had respected him for his solid stance.

"Yes," Chris said, knowing that Hal would have preferred a less decisive response. "It's time."

Hal said nothing for a moment. He closed his eyes. It was the clearest sign of uncontrolled emotion that Chris had ever witnessed from his father-in-law. When a second later Hal opened his eyes, the crystalline blue gaze was again direct and unwavering.

"Yes. You're right, Chris. You'll get no quarrel from me. It's time for all of us to begin to let go." He paused as if considering something, then said, "I'm glad you came to talk about it. It means a lot to me that we're friends. You're important to Liz. And to me, too, of course. I want us to be close...to remain close...think of me as your friend—as your father, if you want. I'd like that. If there's anything I would like, that I'd hope for, it would be that. And, Chris...there's nothing that you can't ask of me or tell me."

It might have been a maudlin speech had it been delivered by someone with less presence than Hal possessed. He was strong enough, sure enough, to be soft. With his silver hair, his strong jaw and the hard, direct gaze, he gave the impression of nobility.

Chris was moved. "Nothing's going to change between us, Hal."

Hal nodded. "I know. We've got too much history together. And Thursday nights—we'd like to count on your visits."

"Sure. Thursday nights stay." Chris was silent for a moment, then took a deep breath and said, "Actually, that's one of the things I wanted to bring up—our Thursday nights. If you wouldn't mind, I'd like to invite Annie to join me this week."

There was a brief hesitation. "I see. I presume, then, that you're getting involved rather quickly."

"I know what you're thinking—"

"She's a very beautiful young woman. It's easy to understand that you would want to have a physical relationship with her. But, uh, speaking purely as your friend, Chris, I'd caution you to—"

"It's more than physical," Chris interrupted. He had spoken more sharply than he had meant to. He modified his initial response, saying, "Thanks for the concern, I appreciate it. It's taken me a long time to adjust to Laura's death. And you're right—before, probably, I might have gotten involved with someone too quickly, too deeply, for all the wrong reasons. Sex being one of them. And loneliness. But this woman...with Annie it's different. It's okay with her, Hal. It's right."

"Fine, fine... I was only offering a bit of objective caution. But if you know your mind, Chris..." Hal's voice trailed off.

"You know, she's still hoping about the painting."

"Starstream?"

"Yes. She was serious about wanting to buy it from you."

"I understand. But Liz and I have a sentimental attachment to it. You know that. We tried to make that clear when she brought the matter up."

Chris nodded. "It reminds Annie of something, too."

"I can't say I understand her passion...with her it actually seems to be an obsession with the painting."

"Maybe it's just the same 'thing' Laura had for the group. She identified with something they represented, I guess."

"Perhaps."

"Do you think that you might consider giving it up for sale? Not now, of course. But sometime...when it's right for you." Chris was speaking euphemistically, knowing Hal would understand. They all had to stop clinging.

"There's always that possibility," Hal said. "Not now, but maybe sometime. And it's only a maybe."

The maybe was good enough. Chris relaxed. He even smiled. "Would you mind if I told her?"

"Don't raise her hopes, Chris."

"No, I wouldn't do that. I'll put it exactly as you said it."

Hal looked at him sharply. "You don't give up when you're on to something." Again, it was not a question, but a statement of fact.

"No," Chris said. "I guess I don't." He definitely wasn't going to give Annie up.

Across from him, Hal's blue eyes had hardened as if he'd thought of something unpleasant.

Chris caught his breath. The moment was over in an instant, but the memory of Hal's brief sign of uncontrolled displeasure was something Chris would not forget. Something was wrong. His intuition and training warned him to pay attention.

But Hal was rising, coming around the desk. "Chris, wish I had more time, but I've got a big-deal meeting with a son of a bitch banker in fifteen minutes. You know how that goes. Nothing I'm looking forward to—the dollar-and-cents grind."

Chris rose, too. "See you on Thursday night. Same time?"

"Same time," Hal said, and walked with him to the door. With a pat to his shoulder, he said, "I wish you all the best with your new lady."

Luck. That's definitely what he needed, Chris thought wryly, as he drove to Annie's from Hal's office. Annie Adderly could be formidably stubborn.

He found her on her front porch. She was seated behind her easel again, so he couldn't make out her mood as he took the path leading to the small cottage. A large bee buzzed passed him, coming too close for comfort, and he stopped momentarily, knowing better than to swat at it.

He heard her radio playing from inside. The music was soft fusion jazz, and it went well with the sunshine and the shadows highlighting the foliage around the house.

"Oh . . . hell!" A ripping sound followed the curse.

Chris saw a wadded ball of paper bounce to the floor, where it joined with other wadded balls.

He began to move forward again. He put an aggressively cheerful tone into his voice, when he started up the steps, saying, "Hi! Fantastic day, isn't it?"

The greeting was met with cold silence. That was okay, too. He had come armed with bold confidence and the fail-safe bait of the Starstream painting.

"Working on something new?" he asked, now coming around to the other side of the easel, where he could see her face clearly. Even clouded and dark, her face was beautiful enough to make his breath catch. God, he thought, feeling weak-kneed in her presence, he wanted this woman.

"Yes," she mumbled, not looking at him. "Something new."

There was a blank piece of paper in front of her, her last effort of the "something new" having been recently hurled to the ground. In her hand she held a charcoal pencil.

"Yeah," Chris said reflectively, pondering her situation. "I feel that way myself sometimes—agitated. When I know something's there, but I can't figure it out, can't quite get my finger on it." His mind skipped to the two murders he was working on, then came back to Annie. "Maybe it's the heat. Want something from inside? Soft drink? Iced tea?" He already knew she was big on iced tea.

Annie shrugged, disinterested.

"Anything I can do to help?" he asked, trying to draw her out of her dark mood.

"With what?" She stared at the blank paper before her. Her hair was piled on top of her head. Some strands had escaped to dangle at her nape and at the sides of her face. He wanted to brush the shiny threads of hair away, wanted to touch her—more than touch her; he wanted to lift her into his arms and take her inside to the bedroom and make love to her for about three days without stopping.

"With anything," Chris said. "Maybe a ride would help. How about a walk. A talk?"

"Chris..." She still would not look at him, merely continued to stare. "I appreciate your concern. Really. But I have to work this through myself." She put the pencil down and brought her knuckles up to both eyes, rubbing furiously, then pressed one fist to her temple.

"Headache?"

She nodded. "Yes, a little. I didn't sleep much last night." She pushed herself from the stool. Standing, she finally looked at him. He saw circles beneath her eyes. "It's not a good time, Chris. I don't mean to be rude."

"Then don't be," he said pleasantly.

Annie smiled. "Everything's so simple for you, isn't it?"

"No. It's not simple at all. Among other things, you're certainly not."

"I don't like being difficult. Really. I know how it must seem to you."

"How must it seem to me?"

"That I'm always touchy and unaccommodating."

"Yeah," he said. "That comes pretty close."

Again, she smiled. "The last time, too. It wasn't good between us, Chris."

"Listen," he said, sensing they were heading into rough seas, "I'd really like something to drink. Mind if I help myself to something? You can just keep—" he glanced at the paper "—tearing off paper." He shrugged and shook his head. "What do I know, anyway? Maybe it's a new art form. You'll be famous for scrunched paper."

He left her standing by a post, looking out to the ocean. A thin mist was gathering out at sea. Catalina Island, twenty-six miles away, was partially obscured in fog. A few sailboats were scudding along the choppy whitecaps raised by the increasing wind. In the far distance an oil tanker heading for San Pedro harbor was slowly cruising along the coast. It was a scene he had looked at a thousand times before, but never with Annie in it. She belonged in his view, as surely as the view belonged in his life. Laguna Beach and Annie were both special, and they were both his.

Chris turned and went inside to the kitchen. It was sparkling clean. He pulled out a couple of glasses from the cabinet and set them on the counter by the sink. On his way to get the tea, which he knew would be in a pitcher in the refrigerator, he passed the back door. His eyes caught the line of plants on the ledge of the small utility porch. What he saw gladdened him. A couple of new plants had been added. He had never believed plants could make him so happy. A person who was going to set off for Mexico in a few days didn't stock up on plants—especially a person like Annie, who cared about living things.

He found the tea on the top refrigerator shelf, poured them both full glasses, replaced the pitcher and was walking out of the kitchen when he stopped short.

For a long moment he just stood there, holding the two glasses in his hand and staring. Then he put the drinks down on the counter and, with a glance toward the front of the house, saw that Annie was busy picking up the papers she had tossed to the ground.

"Chris?" she called. "Could you bring me a paper sack from under the sink when you come back out?"

"Sure! Paper sack. Coming right up."

But he didn't go to the sink.

Instead he moved to the corner of the kitchen, where beside the trash can a canvas had been slashed to pieces with a knife and covered with streaks of black paint. Still, as he held the painting up for examination, it was possible for him to see that before its destruction it had been beautifully executed. From what he could make out, the scene was of the canyon where he had taken Annie. There was a white ranch house in the picture. Yeah...there *was* a house like that; Chris had seen it before himself. She had done a good job, too. The house looked exactly the way she had painted it, only she had managed to catch the house's soul. If a house had such a thing.

Behind him, Chris heard a sound. With the painting in his hand, he turned to find Annie watching him.

Saying nothing, she passed by him and, opening the cabinet under the sink, took out a folded grocery bag.

Neither of them spoke.

Chris put the painting back where he had found it, and taking the glasses, brought them out to the front porch. Annie followed, and after throwing the paper balls into the bag, took her iced tea to the porch railing.

They both sat there, backs against separate posts, facing each other and working on their teas.

He wanted to ask her about the slashed canvas. Whatever had caused her to react so violently worried him. A lot of things were beginning to worry him about this woman with whom he had fallen in love. It was maddening. Love was supposed to feel good.

"I spoke to Hal today," Chris said. He looked out toward the Pacific, but was able to watch Annie's face from the corner of his eye. "He said he might sell the Starstream oil someday."

Annie looked up from nursing her iced tea. "He really said that? He'll sell it to me?"

"There's no guarantee. The key word was 'someday.' But he said there's a possibility. I guess he needs a little more time to let go."

"He understands I'm serious about buying it?"

"Yeah, I'd say he got that loud and clear. In fact, it puzzled him why you're so interested."

"I'm an artist. It's a great painting. And the group was special, too." She spoke rapidly, as if she were making a sales pitch.

Chris wasn't sure he bought it.

But if it were possible that a face could change from sad to happy in the blink of an eye, then Annie's had undergone the metamorphosis. He liked to see her happy, and even though he shouldn't have said it, he added, "It may take a little more time, but I think he'll come around."

"That's great, really great," she said, smiling with genuine happiness.

He felt like a hero, and he liked the feeling.

"I'm going over there on Thursday for dinner," he said.

"You go over every Thursday, don't you?"

"Right. It's a tradition now. It's not anything heavy," he added quickly. It was important that she understand that he was free now. Laura was in the past, and he was living in the present.

"They're good people," Annie said.

"The best."

"And they love you."

"Hal's like a father to me. And a good friend. Definitely. I can tell him anything."

It was just an idle comment, and yet by the expression on Annie's face, he would have thought something terribly significant had been said. She averted her eyes, then turned her face from his view. By the set of her jaw, he could see that she was upset.

"Annie?"

She didn't answer at once.

"Did I say something?"

"No..." Slowly, she turned back to him. Her eyes were glossy, as if she had blinked back tears. "I just thought that it was nice—having someone like that in your life. Someone close. That you could depend on."

"It is nice." He was watching her, trying to understand. He had to tread carefully. "And...and you haven't had anyone like that. Is that it?"

Annie shrugged. "Oh, I've had friends. Good friends," she qualified. "But, no, maybe no one that I could ever completely trust."

He wanted to tell her that he was there, that she could trust him completely. He didn't. Sometimes his first glimpse of her, standing by the parking meter, came back into his mind. She had seemed like a young, frightened doe—about to run if anything came too close to her. If he came on too strong, he would risk losing her.

"I'd like you to come along on Thursday." He all but held his breath.

"I don't know, Chris . . ."

His heart was ready to fall to the pit of his stomach. "Well, I'd like your company, of course. And also, I thought it might be a chance for you to keep in touch with them—about the painting."

Annie was quiet, deep in thought for a few moments. "Okay," she said at last. "Yes, sure. Thursday would be good."

"Fine," said Chris. He could breathe again. His heart was beating at its proper rate. The world had begun to spin.

He felt light-headed as he started down the steps and was already a few feet down the walk when Annie called to him from the porch. She stood at the top of the steps. When he stopped and turned, she came forward, meeting him where he waited.

"Chris . . . about the painting in the kitchen . . ." She stopped, unwilling to say anything further.

He waited, then helped her along. "It looked like you didn't like it."

"I didn't. I didn't like it," she added quickly, as if seizing on his idea.

"I mean, it looks like you *seriously* didn't like it."

Hesitating, she said, "Artistic temperament, I guess."

"It seemed to be more than that," Chris said, and was immediately sorry when at his words Annie seemed to draw away, taking a quick step backward.

"It didn't turn out the way I wanted, that's all," Annie said defiantly.

"Okay," Chris said amiably, trying to cut the tension before it escalated any further and ruined the sunny Thursday, if not his entire life.

"Okay," she agreed, too.

Chris nodded. "So then I'll see you Thursday," he said, and turned. But he now knew for sure that things were anything but "okay."

Chapter Nine

On Thursday night the Haverstroms were polite, if not inordinately warm. Annie and Chris had anticipated their reaction and were prepared for a strained atmosphere, making the best of it by keeping things as light as possible.

The tension was, after all, understandable. This was a milestone in the Haverstroms' lives, the dinner a symbolic acknowledgment of Chris's right to a separate existence. Annie was the physical representation of that change in status.

Liz had made lamb with mint sauce. "Chris's favorite," she said again to Annie, as if she found it important to reassert her proprietary interest in Chris. She set the platter before Hal to carve the roast.

"It smells fabulous," Annie said, because it was true. And to reassure Liz that she hadn't any intention of moving in on her territory, she added, "I'm not really much of a cook myself."

Liz smiled slightly. "Oh, it just takes practice," she said generously. She seemed pleased with Annie's revelation.

The conversation ranged from Hal's business to polite interest in Annie's work. It was Chris who sang her praises, telling the Haverstroms of the gallery show Marge Briskin had planned.

"That's marvelous," Liz said with enthusiasm. "Are you doing any new paintings for it?"

"A few, yes. Marge was hoping to have about twenty to show."

"Laguna's scenery is made for artists. Of course I don't need to tell *you* that. People come from all over the world to paint the coastline. Oh, and you must see the canyon area, too," Liz added. "We've some wonderful views."

"Already done," Chris said. "We went the other day. Annie even began a painting there."

"Oh, really? Good," Liz said with a nod of satisfaction. "Everyone always concentrates on the ocean—which is understandable, but really too bad, because there's a different and equal kind of beauty inland, as well."

"We'd like to see your new work when it's finished," added Hal.

"I'm afraid it won't be," Annie replied. Chris was watching her. She knew she would have to be careful of what she said. "Artistic temperament, I'm afraid. In a fit of despair that I wasn't going to be this century's da Vinci, I destroyed it."

"Oh, no . . . you didn't? Not really . . . ?" Liz said.

"She did, and she shouldn't have," Chris continued purposefully. The brown eyes flashed with energy. "The painting, in spite of the artist's contention, happened to be phenomenal. The canvas all but breathed, the scene was so alive."

Annie had a feeling he was analyzing her as he watched her reaction, dissecting her responses in the same manner as he pored over his cases. Well, if he was on to her, she was equally on to him.

"It was a black mood, and it got the better of me." Annie laughed lightly in an effort to deflect the truth. "Sometimes that happens with us genius artistic types— I guess I should be lucky I still have my ears. Poor van Gogh . . . now *that* was a really bad mood."

"Well, that's a shame about the painting," Liz said, and offered everyone more lamb.

Annie was glad for the distraction. She took an extra helping of meat and even asked for some potatoes, hoping that the conversation was over. But she was wrong, because Hal suddenly took up the subject himself.

"Just out of curiosity, what view did you choose?" Hal wanted to know. He passed on the silver platter of roast potatoes to Chris.

"The . . . uh . . ." She speared a potato, appearing to contemplate it.

". . . view," Chris said helpfully. He was watching her closely.

"It was the . . . there was a hill and, uh . . . I can't remember exactly. A house." Annie's mind began to fill with the image of the white ranch house. Then the vision began to waver as men came into the scene. She could remember the men being there, but beyond that, nothing. The rest was blank.

"There's a lot of pretty scenery back there. Some of it's hard to get to, but you can walk to it, or take the private roads provided that no one shows up to stop you."

It was her turn to respond again.

But no response was forthcoming. She honestly wasn't in a position to elaborate on her outing. The afternoon that Chris had found her on the porch, surrounded by failed attempts to begin a new project, she had slashed the painting out of helpless rage. Again and again she had struggled to remember the details of her visit to the canyon, only to succumb to a blinding fear.

Now three people were watching her, waiting for her to say something.

"I—I..." She started to recall the shadowy image of a man's face, and then her mouth went dry and tears filled her widened eyes. "Would you excuse me," she said suddenly, and pushed herself up from the table and bolted toward the door leading from the dining room into the hall.

"Are you all right?" she heard Liz's concerned voice call after her, and then Hal's voice echoing the question.

Chris said nothing, but she could feel his eyes following her as she moved swiftly through the room, over the white carpet and into the hall. She needed the safety of more distance. Her heels clicked over the white travertine marble as she sought the relief a moment's privacy would bring.

Locking the door to the powder room, she leaned against the door, her heart hammering. In the mirror her eyes appeared as round and large as saucers. She stared at herself, trying in vain to recall the events that had upset her so greatly, but it was no use. She was held captive by her own mind.

A moment passed, and then she heard a gentle rapping on the door. "Annie?" It was Chris checking on her. "Everything okay?"

"Fine," she called through the closed door. "Sorry for running out like that. A little dizzy, I guess. From the wine. Maybe the heat and the wine. I didn't eat much today. Okay now." And she ran some water in the sink. It was a nice normal sound. It also served to cut off their conversation.

When she returned, she was outwardly calm, taking her seat again and bringing her water glass to her lips as she listened to the discussion in progress. The subject had turned to Chris's job.

"You're all right?" Liz asked with concern as soon as Annie was seated.

"Oh, yes. Sorry to have interrupted...I'm fine now. I just felt a bit dizzy. Maybe too much wine." Of course, that was unlikely. She had had only one glass of white wine, and it was still half full. But maybe no one had counted.

Then she looked at Chris, who was looking at her, and his dark, skeptical eyes said that he didn't buy her story. Chris noticed everything; he noticed too much. But Hal was asking him about his work, and it was necessary for Chris to respond.

"We have the computers, of course," Chris said, answering Hal. "But we also keep all the cases in three-ring binders. Murder books, we call them."

"Colorful term," said Hal, half laughing. "If not a touch gruesome."

"Apt. They never go out of print, either."

"You mean the cases are always open—like Jim's murder?"

"Right. There's no statute of limitations on the time required to solve a murder."

"Comforting, I suppose—that society places such a high value on human life," Hal commented thoughtfully. "One begins to wonder, reading the headlines these days. But realistically, what can you expect to find after so many years?"

Chris sipped his wine. "Odd as it may seem, plenty sometimes. When you get farther away, you pick up a new perspective. Something totally unexpected can pop into your head—some crazy, small detail. But that can be it. Just one little word, one loose thread…something you see, or something seemingly innocent that someone says. And that's the missing piece to the puzzle." He looked directly at Annie, as if sending her a message only she would understand. "It's happened before," Chris said, this time turning his attention to Hal.

"Often?" Liz asked. She seemed rapt. It was clear that she adored Chris.

"Not often. But it does occur." And Chris went on to recount three cases in which it had happened.

For Annie, it was fascinating—and troubling—listening to him talk, catching a glimpse of how his mind worked. At times he seemed dogmatic, and at other times creative; the two traits didn't usually fit well together.

Hal must have also considered Chris's mental acuity, for a few minutes later he interrupted an entirely different conversation, saying, "You know, Chris, the offer still stands for you to come on board at my company. You'd start at the top, of course—taking over the presidency. And I'd move up to chairman of the board. With your mind and my experience, we'd take over the world—at the very least Southern California. Can I tempt you?''

Chris shook his head. "Come on, Hal. You flatter me. You know as well as I do, I don't know a beam from a hammer."

Annie respected him for both his humility and the show of independence. Any other man would have jumped at the opportunity Hal Haverstrom was offering, a guarantee of wealth, security and power.

"No problem. You don't need to know the nuts-and-bolts stuff," responded Hal in a pleasant voice of honeyed persuasion, but the blue eyes were fixed in hard concentration. "Grunts can know all that. You'd be working on finance and marketing. You're brilliant, Chris. Native intelligence. And devastating charm. It would make me proud—and secure—to have you head the operation. Name your price. Go on…play around, test me. I promise you, the sky's not too high."

Chris smiled, looking down at his plate, and shook his head. "Hal…thanks, but I like the snoop business."

"Okay. That's how you feel tonight. And before. But there's always tomorrow. Think about it, Chris. I see this working out for both of us."

Hal and Liz would have liked them to stay longer, but an hour after dinner Chris said they had to be leaving. There was an awkward moment of silence—the evening was still early—and then Hal stood up from the sofa, and so did Liz, and Annie followed suit.

A half hour later they took the stairs up to the second-floor jazz club in a renovated building on Pacific Coast Highway. The owner knew Chris, and so, apparently, did quite a few other people there. Annie felt their eyes follow her as Chris led the way to a small round table in the back of the room.

Chris ordered them both drinks—white wine for Annie, a Scotch for himself. When the waitress brought the wine, Annie didn't say anything. She knew Chris would never have ordered the wine for her if he had bought her earlier story about being dizzy.

"Hal's right," Annie said, leaning close to Chris to compensate for the loudness of the music being played by the trio at the far end of the room. "You could do anything. When you were describing how you unraveled that case with the man who had blown up the boat and claimed himself as dead, then murdered his ex-wife . . . let's say I gained a whole lot more insight into who I'm out with."

Chris laughed and took a long drink. Turning to Annie, he said, "And the charm? What about the charm Hal mentioned?"

"Yeah," she said, meeting his direct gaze. "That's there, too. Definitely."

"It doesn't seem to help me with you."

"Oh, I'm charmed, all right. More than charmed," Annie confessed lightly, but with more feeling than was comfortable for her.

"And that's the problem, isn't it?"

"Yes—you're too devastatingly attractive. I'm afraid I'll lose you to the admiring hordes—"

"You're afraid of closeness." He wasn't playing anymore.

She pressed her nose against his for an instant and, leaning back, said in jest, "There. You see—close. I'm totally fearless."

But Chris was not to be deterred. "I thought I was the one who had to work at getting close. So it seems we have at least one thing in common."

Annie felt her stomach turn over. She had had this conversation too many times before. "I don't think you really know me well enough to come to that conclusion." She sounded cold.

"Which is precisely my point, isn't it? You won't let me know you. You won't let anyone get near you. Or maybe I'm wrong. Am I wrong? Your cat—Muffin gets close. That's all that I can see when it comes to intimate relationships. But maybe I'm just being shortsighted. Maybe you *have* let someone get close to you, and that's why you're running now."

He had been talking fast. At his last statement, Annie flinched. Chris saw the response, too. He had been waiting for a reaction.

"I don't understand what you're talking about, Chris," she said quickly.

"Okay, I'll make it easy to understand. Is there someone else in your life, Annie? Or was there? Maybe someone who hurt you?"

And then she understood. He wasn't deliberately hunting for skeletons in her closet, he was just jealous. She almost laughed out of relief. "No . . . no, there's no one else. There hasn't been anyone," she qualified, and hoped that this would satisfy him.

Chris didn't look convinced. He studied her, staring hard. "You're a beautiful woman, Annie. It strains credulity that you haven't been seriously involved with anyone."

"I've made it a point never to get entwined that way. My work's always been—"

"Oh, come on. Don't give me that free-spirit-artist-spiel again. You're flesh and blood. The kind of fire you've got in you, Annie... Your nature isn't going to let you settle for paint on canvas, not completely, anyway."

"I'm telling you the truth," she said, and because it was, in fact, the truth, her voice held conviction. She just hadn't told him the whole story.

Chris paused, weighing thoughts of his own. Then he said, "Okay. Let's say I'll buy the fairy tale. So you've kept yourself in an ivory tower of your own construction. But that doesn't explain other things."

The music being played by the trio was gaining in tempo. She raised her glass of wine and downed a quarter of it in one long swallow. Chris's hand closed over hers, as she brought it back to the table.

"Nervous?" he asked, piercing her with his dark eyes. "Why are you always so nervous when we talk about you?"

She held her ground, able to meet his stare with her own. "I'm not nervous. I just don't understand why every time we get together, I have to undergo an interrogation."

"Nothing adds up," Chris returned, sounding every bit as frustrated with the situation he found himself in. "Who fixed the wheel, Annie? Why did you slash the painting when it was so good?"

"I don't know who fixed the wheel. And I told you—I didn't like the way the painting looked. That it's so good is your opinion, but I think as the artist I'm entitled to my own notions of what works and what doesn't. Art's very subjective, and these were my feelings. I would appreciate it if you'd back off, Chris. I'm not a suspect in one of your murder cases."

"Look, I care about you," Chris said fervently. "I don't want to see you unhappy. Or hurt in any way. Laguna Beach attracts a lot of weirdos. It's only natural that in my line of work, I tend to worry about things that don't add up."

The music was now driving toward a climactic crescendo. Annie felt as if she were caught in a whirlwind of words and notes and feelings.

"Can we get out of here?" she asked, trying not to sound as desperate as she felt.

Chris paid the tab for the drinks, and a minute later they were walking along the boardwalk, a light offshore breeze rustling their clothes and tossing their hair. The tension was still there between them, spoiling what should have been a wonderful evening.

Annie stopped. Chris took a couple of steps ahead, then turned. They looked at each other for a long moment, both feeling the other's unhappiness along with their own.

"I wanted this night to be good for us. Not like...like it's turned out," Chris said.

He looked melancholy and beautiful in the moonlight, the planes of his face shimmering in the filtered light from a nearby street lamp. His waist was small, the shoulders broad. She could remember the feel of the powerful legs; she could recall the rhythm when they had moved urgently against her own, driving his passion. And the very memory made her shiver, made her experience all the more her inflexible isolation.

If she could bend just a bit, just enough to be close to him again, to come out of the cold and into the warmth of his love—of *their* love. How dangerous could that be?

Very dangerous. But, yes, she did love him.

She loved him.

The admission hit her like a hard slap in the face. She *loved*.

There was an instant of shock, as if the wind had been suddenly knocked from her lungs, and then a sense of joy spread through her entire being—her flesh, her soul, her very bones. Love existed. Love was real. Love was in her, of her, surrounding her—but only because she had let Chris into that circle of love.

She felt light and free. And the love made her brave, willing to dare....

"Chris, I want to get close...really. I *am* close!" she burst out, caught up in the discovery of her own feelings. "I've never wanted any man so much as I want you." She was crying from the joy of being able to say the words.

"Oh, Annie...you've *got* me." He closed the distance separating them and swept her into his arms, squeezing her, kissing her deeply, hungrily. They were losing themselves in that kiss, finding each other. The world no longer existed. There was only the two of them lost to the need of the other's desire.

He was hard against her, and she felt the rush of his desire through his fingers as he caressed her back, lowering his hands to follow the outline of her hips and the curve of her buttocks. "Let's go home," he said, and his voice was rough with passion.

And then, a thought occurred to him, and he turned his head to the side and said, "A better idea." He kissed her again, and then urging her along, they set off.

He led her quickly down the sand, where both of them ran like children, carrying their shoes. On fire, they came together and kissed and touched, wild with need and joy and love.

They didn't have far to run, and soon found themselves on the outskirts of the small, quaint village.

Their destination turned out to be a door set into a natural rock wall that climbed straight up from the sand. Above one cliff was a plateau where the lights from an old frame house shone in the windows. The glow fell softly upon the beach where Annie and Chris stood.

"A friend's family owns this place," Chris said as he jimmied the lock with a pick blade of a Swiss Army knife he pulled from his pocket. "David—my buddy— calls it his meditation cave. We come here sometimes with a six-pack and talk about the meaning of life. His folks rent the upstairs out—the house, that is—to tourists for *beaucoup* bucks. It's near the center of town and on the beach and never mind that the plumbing's archaic, they can pull down $2,000 a week."

The door was open, and Chris entered first, searching around in the dark until he reached what he obviously knew he'd find—a candlestick and matches. Annie entered the small room after him.

The yellow and rust earth tones of the natural rock glowed in the magical light. The air was close at first, but Chris opened a small casement window set high on the outside wall, and the fresh scent of sea air blew through the open door and window.

The interior was neat and clean, not more than ten by ten feet in size, and furnished with cast-off furnishings. There was a small bed, barely wide enough for two people. It was covered with blankets, and a stack of clean sheets was folded at the end. Against the far wall, opposite the door, was a bookshelf with yellowed editions of paperbacks and some old magazines, a few ceramic decorative pieces of the tourist variety and finally on the right side of the room, a tiny oak table with two straightback chairs that had seen better days.

The candle flickered, almost blowing out, and Chris closed the door against the breeze. After turning the lock, he faced her with the candle in his hand. "I've never brought anyone here before—if that's what's crossing your mind."

"It was," Annie said with a smile. "Quite a setup for a moonlit walk."

"Then you don't know me..."

It made her sad to hear him say it, and suddenly she wanted more than anything to tell him her whole life's story.

But he was walking toward her then, placing the candle on the table, taking her into his arms, kissing her mouth, her eyes, her neck. From the window, a cool gust circled through the room, and she felt the cold air on her breasts hardening her nipples as Chris slid down the bodice of her sun-dress. His mouth was hungry on her skin, teasing, tasting, burning her with his tongue. Almost unable to breathe from the pleasure, she twined her hands in his thick dark hair and let him torture her.

The skirt slid to the floor, and the thin nylon of her bikini pants followed in a whisper as Chris pressed his face against her stomach and pulled her body hard against him.

Behind them the small window creaked under the force of another gust. The candle flickered.

Chris lifted her and carried her to the bed, then ripped off his clothes as his eyes burned down the length of her form, unclothed and supine on the narrow bed. Outside, there was the sound of distant laughter, like the sound of far-off bells in some high, remote village.

He moved slowly, deliberately, like a sleek cat, every muscle like silk flowing. In the soft yellow glow, he moved slowly to her....

Down he came, his body brushing lightly over hers, his torso suspended, taut, hard, ready to join with her. But he would not give in to the pleasure that soon.

For Annie it was all pleasure. Touching him was pleasure. Feeling him stiffen and tremble as she closed her fingers over him was her ecstasy as well as his. The sound of his voice was deep and raspy as he fought against losing control.

Like Chris, she wanted the time to last and last.

And then, together in their need, they joined completely, becoming one body, then one soul. Shuddering, Chris cried out in an agony of pleasure, even as she arched toward the pinpoint of bright, hot light she rose to meet. For an instant she was alone, lost even to her own self. Then rising with Chris again, she was brought to ecstasy a second time, and then held as she fell to earth slowly, gently, whispering his name, touching his body slick with moisture, damp with their love.

"I love you," she whispered. "I love you...." And she fell asleep in that certainty, curled in his arms, feeling the strength of his body as a protective shield surrounding her forever.

Chapter Ten

Jeff Parker stood beside him at the site of the canyon murder. That's what they were already calling it in the department—the canyon murder. It had been two days since the body had been discovered. The time of the victim's death had been determined as two days prior to that. Chris thought back. The painting Annie had slashed had been done on that same day, at this same place.

"So what do you think?" Jeff asked.

Chris didn't answer at once. His thoughts were on the painting. He remembered the shadows, the direction of the sun as it hit the house. Annie's style augmented the realism of the moment, capturing an exaggerated interpretation of her subject matter and making the ordinary appear fantastic.

"What time of day did the murder occur?" Chris asked Jeff.

"The coroner says late eleven-ish, give or take a few minutes."

Chris looked at the sun. It was ten-thirty, and the shadows around the house were slightly off from the way they had appeared in Annie's painting. Given another hour or so, the sun would shift, showing the scene pretty much the way Annie had captured it on her canvas.

Turning around slowly, he scanned the area. It was reasonably easy to estimate where Annie must have set up her easel.

"I'm going to take a walk," Chris said, and left Jeff to talk to another officer combing the surroundings for clues.

He walked around for a few minutes, studying distance and angles from the perspective Annie had had of the scene. If she had been there during the time of the murder, then she would have had a clear, unobstructed view of the front of the house and part of the driveway.

Chris waited at the crime scene, doing his part in the investigation as best he could while at the same time keeping the most important piece of information the department had on the murder to himself. There was a witness to the crime.

At 11:52 a.m. what had been a solid suspicion in Chris's mind became a solid fact. He stood at the top of the small knoll, looking down at the house with the shadows just as they had appeared in Annie's painting. No doubt about it; Annie had been at the scene of the crime when the murder had been committed. Annie had seen something. She had been terrified, had run and once home, had endured some sort of flashback that caused her to destroy the physical representation of what she had witnessed.

That made sense. But what didn't add up was why she would have kept the matter to herself?

There was no chance that she herself might have been involved in the killing—Chris wouldn't accept that possibility, not personally or professionally. Annie simply wasn't a criminal. She was warm and caring and gentle and sensitive, and that was precisely what made the matter all the more puzzling.

An unearthly shiver passed through Chris. The only logical reason was the assumption that Annie was afraid.

That Annie might be in danger catapulted Chris off the knoll and to the far side of the driveway where his car was parked. As he did a U-turn in the direction of the main road, he saw Jeff Parker watching him from the front stoop of the ranch house.

Jeff was going to have questions later, and for the first time in their long and close relationship, Chris didn't know if he was going to be able to answer his best friend truthfully. The most important thing in his life was to protect Annie, and he knew as he sped down Laguna Canyon Road that he would do anything it took to keep her safe.

Catching sight of her sitting serenely on her front porch fifteen minutes later made his heart pound to a frantic beat.

"Chris..." Her blue eyes were lit with happiness as he moved up the walk to the house. She had on a light blue summer dress, her hair loose to her shoulders, and wore no shoes, the sandals having been kicked to one side of the rocking chair on which she sat. Muffin was cradled in her arms.

The scene was a living portrait, delicate and pure. A shaft of light filtered through the branches of a eucalyptus, illuminating her perfect skin.

The sight brought Chris's thoughts as far from murder as it was possible to go. And that made the situation all the more awful. Because such beauty was so quickly obliterated, so fragile, so undefended against the darker realities.

Annie had risen from the chair as he'd made his way up the steps to her. Muffin was still in her arms. He heard the cat's gentle purr, soft and pleasing in the noonday quiet.

"What a surprise," she said, her lips curved gently upward. "If I'd known, I would have made something for lunch."

Muffin, disturbed from her comfort, squirmed out of Annie's arms and leaped softly to the floor.

It was anguish having to face the radiant happiness in her eyes as she reached for him. He had come to kill her pleasure, not to revel in it. "I didn't know, either," Chris said.

They stood close, and he knew that she expected him to kiss her. Wanting her, and feeling like Judas, he reached out and brought her roughly against him. He twined his fingers in her hair and held her shoulders with more pressure than was normal as he kissed her hard. It was a kiss of passion and futility and fear. When he finally relaxed his hold, she was looking at him in confusion.

"What is it?" she asked worriedly, searching his face. "What's wrong?"

"What did you see in the canyon that day, Annie? What did you see that day when you did the painting of the house?"

Her face paled. "That again?"

"A man was shot, killed in the house you painted. And I've every reason to believe the murder occurred at the time you were in the area."

For an instant she appeared to be in shock. "Murder?"

"The guy who owned the place..."

"That's...that's awful." She turned her face to the side, deep in thought as she looked past the porch. When she turned back, she said, "What's this all about, Chris? You can't think I'm involved."

"I think you saw something, that you know something."

Her color had still not returned. There were red splotches on her cheeks, where the skin had been drained of its natural glow. "I don't," she said. "I went there to paint. That was all. I don't know anything about murders."

"What upset you that day?"

"Upset...? I don't know what you mean?"

"The painting, Annie. You destroyed the painting—"

"Oh. I told you."

"You violently destroyed what anyone else, including myself, would consider a beautiful landscape painting."

"Chris, we went through all that. In excruciating detail, as I recall. Artistic tantrums are an occupational hazard of the profession. If that's too simple, and your complicated mind just can't accept anything that mundane, then I can't help it." She turned and reached for the screen door. "I wish you'd just leave it be and get off my back with the questions, Chris."

Chris reached forward and grabbed her arm. He spun her around to face him. "It also goes with the territory of *my* profession to play the Grand Inquisitor. It's my job to solve murders, Annie."

She wrenched her arm free and jerked open the screen door. Chris followed after her, entering the living room hard on her heels.

Annie whirled around. "I don't like this," she said vehemently.

"I like it even less," Chris shot back. "But I don't have a choice. I've got to ask questions, Annie, and until I get some sort of solid answers, I can't let things rest."

"I didn't see a murder," she said, fixing steady blue eyes on him.

"Okay," Chris said. "So you didn't see the murder itself. But you may have seen something else...someone else. Don't you understand? I'm not hounding you because I want to make things rough on you."

"Well, you sure haven't brightened my day any. You're telling me you don't believe me."

"I'm trying to protect you. And someone else who might become another victim. I don't have any motive as to why anyone would want this guy dead. For all I know this could have been done by some nut, and that nut is out there this very minute, a time bomb just waiting to go off again." He fell quiet for a moment. Then, moving to the front window, he looked out at the Pacific far below and said, "And if you saw someone, then that someone might have also seen you, Annie. That means that you could be in danger."

He didn't turn around to see her face. It wasn't necessary. With a sick feeling in his gut, he knew he was right.

Finally she said, "I don't remember what I saw."

Chris looked over his shoulder, surprised. "You don't remember? But you *did* see something—"

"I don't know," she said. "Really." She started for the kitchen. "You want something to eat? There's a little ham—"

"No," Chris said. "I can't let this go, Annie."

"Why?" she demanded, suddenly turning on her heels. She faced him with a look of fury mixed with anguish. "I told you I can't remember anything. When you keep pushing me, it...it—" And she brought both her hands to both sides of her head. "This hurts me, Chris. I feel attacked...confused."

"I'm sorry. I don't mean to confuse you, and I certainly don't want to attack you. That's the last thing I want, Annie. But I've got to find answers. No matter what," he said quietly.

She dropped her hands limply to her sides. "Then I don't want to see you now."

"I'll have to come back," he said softly.

"Then it will have to be on official business," she said coldly.

"I love you, Annie." And then he turned and left.

Chapter Eleven

I love you." Chris's parting words echoed in Annie's head as she passed through the silent living room.

A silvery flash caught her eye, and tensing, she turned her head quickly.

It was nothing; only her own image reflected in the oval mirror suspended over a narrow drop-leaf table. She stopped and moved closer, staring in unhappy fascination at the picture she presented.

Her face was dead white.

Maybe, she thought, that was because she felt as if she were dying.

"I love you," came the echo of Chris's words.

And from within her a voice cried back, "I love *you*!"

The blue eyes in the mirror stared back at her, round and large and sorrowful. *What did you see?* she asked of them silently, desperately. *What did you see at the canyon?*

In answer, a flicker passed behind the blue surface as distant memories surged to the surface, attempting to escape the dark prison of her mind.

From the mist of her memory, the image of a man's face appeared. The features were almost distinguishable...but not quite. The eyes became clearer, blue eyes like her own. And then the mouth as he started to speak.

She strained to hear.

And blackness closed in on her: the veil, the man, everything was gone. As usual.

She stood at the mirror, gripping the edge of the small table in front of it. Her knuckles were white. Pain seared her soul.

She did not know how long she stood there. Abruptly, the sound of the telephone at the other side of the room brought her into the real world again.

Stumbling toward the shrilling bell, Annie grabbed for the phone. A surge of relief filled her. Chris had felt her despair. He was calling to save her, to waken her from the nightmare.

Joy pumped through her veins as she brought the receiver to her ear. She imagined his face, his beautiful, handsome face, as she smiled and said, "Hello...?"

"Annie..." came the excited female voice. "Have I got some news for you."

"Oh." Annie sank into a chair near the phone. "Marge..." She wanted to cry, and bit her upper lip.

"Listen, I want to tell you in person, okay? So, you've *got* to come down here. I can't leave the store now."

Annie's eyes filled with tears. "Marge . . . I'm really not feeling much like going out right now."

"No...absolutely no, Annie. Do whatever it takes to get it together, and come on down here. This is *important*, Annie. It's going to change your entire life."

There was no chance to object further. Marge had hung up.

Leaving Annie's house, Chris was more alone than ever. He felt bereft of both the joyful present and the familiar past with its mixture of fond memories and pain.

How quickly things changed.

He had entered Annie's house, filled with purpose and the conviction that he would protect her from all danger. Instead, he had discovered that the true enemy lay within Annie herself. He, who would risk his own life to save the woman he loved, could do nothing on her behalf.

Still willing to fight lions and tigers, he was not in the frame of mind to spar verbally with Jeff, who would have a host of questions and unwanted opinions.

Instead of returning to the department, Chris retreated to his home, where he cast off his shirt and shoes, and called into the office to leave the message for Jeff that he wouldn't be back that day.

Unfortunately, he couldn't get off that easy. Jeff grabbed the telephone while the departmental assistant scrounged around for a memo pad.

Jeff must have been waiting like a vulture for him to return.

"So what's the deal, Farrentino?"

"No deal. I won't be back in till tomorrow. I've got some thinking to do."

"What do you have going on this canyon murder thing?"

"Nothing. That's why I'm cutting out. I need some space to think about things."

"Bull."

"Look, Jeff...I'm not sure of anything right now."

"Bull," he repeated. "I know you, Farrentino. You were on to something when you were having your little climb around the location."

There was silence between the two partners. Then Chris said, "You can't help me on this, Jeff."

"What? Since when are you the Lone Ranger?" Jeff sounded frustrated, hurt and angry.

And Chris didn't blame him. But there was Annie to consider. It could very well be critical to her welfare—not to mention their own relationship—that he not offer her up as fodder for the investigative mill.

Jeff was still waiting for a response, and Chris said, "Since now, Jeff."

"I don't like the way this sounds."

"I don't like it, either. But that's the way it's got to be."

When he hung up, he sank into his easy chair, certain now that he wasn't going to be able to protect Annie for very long.

He had already mentioned Annie's presence at the site of the murder scene to Hal and Liz. He had no way of knowing who Liz or Hal had spoken to about the matter.

From past experience he knew a tangled knot would sooner or later present itself to view. Covering up for Annie would never work.

The quiet familiarity of the den cocooned him, drawing him back to a less complex time in his life. A box sat on the floor, filled with some of Laura's child-hood artifacts. He had meant to carry the box out to the garage; now he was glad he hadn't. Rather than de-pressing him, he felt cheered by its presence. He smiled, thinking of her small hands playing with the dolls, the small dishes, the box of Pick-up-Sticks. And then, piled beside the box, the stack of picture albums. He picked them up and began leafing through days that were sim-pler than the one he presently lived.

With a certain degree of surprise, he found himself soothed by the memorabilia that had been so impor-tant to Laura.

For two hours he read and reread the news clippings and magazine articles detailing the lives and careers of the Starstream members. Pictures of the famous musi-cians caught his imagination, making him wonder how so many, Annie and Laura included, could be obsessed with people who were no more than strangers.

Finally he came to the series of articles and graphic photographs chronicling the accident that claimed the lives of everyone in the band—or rather, almost every-one.

A little girl, the daughter of the band's lead singer and his wife, had survived.

Chris studied the pictures and reread the articles, re-calling how Laura had been affected by the story of the little girl—Canaan—who had been left behind with her mother's friend. She was to have been picked up later by the mother. The child was eight then, almost the same age as Laura had been when the tragedy had oc-curred.

Troubled, Chris found himself reading the articles a third time. And then he understood the source of his confusion; it was the name Canaan.

Canaan was the signature on Hal's painting. The little girl had apparently grown up and become an artist. It was she who had painted the bus that hung in his in-laws' house. No wonder the painting radiated so much power. Love and regret colored the oils. As an artist herself, Annie must have identified with the kinds of emotions that had generated the work's brilliant execution.

He read further.

One other man had survived the crash, Starstream's drummer, Corrie Bonner. Bonner had been with the group almost from the beginning, and had been fired just the night before, which was why he wasn't on the bus when it had crashed.

Following that story, Chris studied the picture of Corrie Bonner displayed with the caption "Hunted for Love." It was the title of one of the group's biggest hits, and also a play on the fact that Bonner was being sought as a prime suspect in the deaths of the Starstream members.

On numerous occasions Bonner had fixed the bus when it had had mechanical problems. It was also common knowledge that Bonner and Michelle Palance had once been lovers. Later she had married Rod Palance. Bonner's firing was seen as the motive for the rigging of the tragic accident. He was subsequently wanted for questioning by the police. A warrant for his arrest had been issued, but had never been served. Bonner had fled, and the case had never been closed.

Chris himself could buy the theory of Bonner's having committed the crime.

An hour later, while stocking up on groceries in the market, Chris was still plagued by the lack of real answers in the articles.

In the dairy department he reached for a carton of milk, and found himself standing there a minute later, his hand extended with his fingers still wrapped around the container. Something was amiss.

He told himself to forget it; looking through Laura's things had served only to upset him.

But back at home, he found he could not get rid of the conflicting images. It was an hour later before he could reach Jeff, who was off duty and had been out at the shooting range with some of the other cops.

"Yeah?" Jeff answered from his home phone, sounding out of breath.

"Hey," Chris said, "you remember that group Starstream?"

"Yeah, sure," Jeff answered, breathing heavily. "I know them. What do you think, I live under a rock? Starstream—they're all dead. Years ago."

"Not all of them are dead," Chris said. "The drummer's still alive. Somewhere."

"Okay. So?"

"I'm wondering what happened to him."

"I don't have enough to worry about right here, right now? I've got to worry about some music dude from way back, huh?"

"He's alive, he's somewhere, and he's crazy."

"What else is new, Farrentino?"

"Word has it that he was responsible for the death of the whole group."

"I remember. It was just a rumor."

"He disappeared. No one ever really knew for sure. But it looks like it had to be him."

"Well, it's always gotta be somebody. You know, I'm sweating like a pig. I've gotta take a shower. Hey, get this, Farrentino... I beat out Korminski at the range—

thirty-two dead-center bull's-eyes against his twenty-eight."

"This was one of the most famous music groups in American history, and one day they disappeared over a cliff, and the guy who cut the brakes went scot-free."

Jeff sighed deeply. "Okay, okay. I get the picture. This was a major tragedy, followed by a great injustice, and we've got one more unsolved murder on the books along with a million other unsolved crimes. I can't get worked up over this. I just want to go and get my shower, okay?"

"And I want to know where he is."

"Why the fixation, Farrentino?"

"I'm not sure. Maybe it's personal—I just don't know. Laura was really attached to the group. And Annie, too."

"So you want to be a hero and catch the guy who made them cry, huh? Pretty far out, Farrentino. You need more than a badge. You need a suit of armor. Or maybe you need your head examined."

"Probably the latter," Chris said, and he wasn't laughing. "The guy's name—the drummer—was Corrie Bonner, just in case something clicks along the way. You know how it is...you never know when something comes up. I'm going to do some computer checking tomorrow. I have an old buddy from the FBI school who's working homicide in the district where the case went down. I can't do anything official, but I can do it off the record. And I thought if you have the time, you could—"

"In case it slipped your mind, Lancelot, the canyon story's breaking in the newspapers tomorrow. We're going to be up to our cerebellums in calls from crazies and reporters, not to mention our favorite garden-variety hysterics who'll be thinking there's a maniac loose behind every bush and why don't we do something about it. This Corrie Bonner creep just isn't going to be a high priority number on my immediate list of things to do. Catch my drift?''

"Sure. Just so he's somewhere on your list...." He began to lower the phone.

"Chris?"

"Yeah, what?"

"Are you, uh, doing okay?"

"I'm fine." He hesitated, wanting to say more. "Catch you tomorrow..."

No, he wasn't doing okay. He was losing Annie's love, and beyond that he had to worry about her losing her life. If she had seen someone commit a murder, then that person may have seen her. He felt totally helpless. And in love.

Maybe that was the worst of it . . . the love.

Marge Briskin was with a couple when Annie entered the gallery. They were looking at one of her own paintings, deciding if they could afford the price.

And that's how Annie got her news.

"There are very few times when a dealer can honestly say a painting by a new artist is an investment. This is one time when it's a certainty. The artist has just been awarded a fully supported grant by the Farbinger Foundation to study art abroad for two years. It's the most prestigious award of its kind in the world. At least two thousand artists compete, and those must have certified dealers or recognized members of the art community to recommend their work. The artist selected for this distinction is guaranteed fame of an international stature. Frankly, if I had to sell my blood to own this work, I'd do it." She glanced over at Annie, who was staring at her, stunned. Marge grinned. "How would you like to meet the artist?" she asked.

And amid smiles, the sale was made.

"Well, congratulations," Marge said, beaming as she walked over to Annie once the excited couple had departed with their investment. "Before long, I'm sure we'll have a few Adderlys in the Whitney."

"I don't know what to say. This is . . . I mean, I can't believe it. Is this *real*?"

"Absolutely?"

"But how—?"

"Me. I did it. I know it sounds crazy, and it was. I can hardly believe the whole thing myself. The deadline was two days away for submissions to the Farbinger Foundation. But a friend of mine with the Getty Museum had some pull with the acceptance committee. He came down last week and went absolutely crazy when he saw your work—and insisted to the committee that you were to be included in the running. Photographs were submitted of your other paintings, and one I told you was sold—well, actually that was the one I sent special air to New York City. They saw. They judged. They awarded. You are numero uno, baby. Three weeks from today you'll be packed and on your way to fame and fortune."

"I don't know what to say. It's so incredible. Marge, how can I thank you?"

"Oh, that's easy." Marge drew out the "easy" and laughed. "Just let me be your exclusive dealer for the first five years, and if I do well, then we'll talk about another five years. Fair?"

"More than fair," Annie said. "Can I sit down? I've got to sit down." She stumbled over to a low, blue silk upholstered loveseat, generally used for customers to view paintings at their leisure. At first she was merely stunned by the good fortune. Then her heart began to beat like a hummingbird's wings. It was hard to accept such good fortune.

"Paris...Florence...Rome...Madrid," Marge listed aloud, using a finger for each city. "You'll have the best teachers, the most fantastic sites available to you. All your lodging will be free, along with a spending allowance and—can you believe it?—a salary."

"They're paying me to—"

"—do what you love."

Love? Annie stared at Marge, not seeing her, not hearing her. All she could think of was Chris. She couldn't leave Chris. Chris and the cottage and Laguna Beach and Marge—no, there wasn't enough fame and fortune in the whole world to make up for the loss of these people and places she loved. All of a sudden yesterday's tiff was unimportant. The possibility of losing Chris's love put everything else in life in clear perspective; nothing was as important as love.

"...come over to see you, maybe in December if my husband can get away. Of course, I'm a liberated woman, and could just jet over there on my—"

"I can't," Annie said. Her voice was so soft that even she could hardly hear it.

"What?" Marge asked, her eyes wide in disbelief.

"I can't take it," Annie said, looking up at Marge, whose face had suddenly turned to stone.

Then in the next instant Marge had relaxed and was saying, "Oh, Annie... you're just afraid. It's natural. Lots of people have trouble reaching their potential because it's really a scary thing to leave the comforts of home and dive into the unknown.''

Annie rose from the low bench and moved to stand before one of the canvases—not her own—hanging on the wall. The scene was of Laguna Beach. Looking at it, she could feel the pulse of the town, smell the ocean blowing off the Pacific, and there, high in the green hills, was a cottage where she belonged. For a moment she studied it in silence, weighing her feelings for Chris and Laguna against a future holding glory and loneliness.

"I'm not afraid of success," she said at last.

"Please don't tell me it doesn't matter. That you paint only for the deep fulfillment your art brings you. I won't stand for that kind of baloney."

"Of course the grant matters, and I don't have anything against making money. But other things matter more."

"Name one thing."

Annie turned, facing Marge fully again.

"Oh," Marge said, her eyes widening. "Oh. I get it now. You're in love? You're in *love*," she said firmly the second time.

Annie felt herself coloring. Her heart swelled, and she felt happy and giddy at the same time, just to be able to admit the truth aloud. She felt like other people now—she could live in the light and not the shadows; she wasn't about to take off down the highway just when she'd gotten close to someone.

"Let me guess?" Marge said, narrowing her eyes. "I know...I've got it. It's Chris? Chris Farrentino. Hal and Liz's Chris Farrentino..."

Annie nodded. "I met him there. No, I met him first by a parking meter. Then later I met him more formally at the Haverstroms'." It was hard not to smile; just hearing his name made her warm all over. "I've never been in love before."

Marge sighed. "Ah, love..." She shook her head, and rolling her eyes, looked to the ceiling. "Why, oh why, God, did it have to be now that this woman had to fall in love?" She looked back at Annie. "Dear girl, destiny has knocked, greatness has come a-calling. Do you know that thousands of women burned their Maidenforms just so that you could be afforded this once-in-a-lifetime opportunity to attain professional recognition, possibly even immortality? And you are going to throw it all away for something as socially regressive as love?" She paused. "Look, I'm all for passion. Don't misunderstand. I still get a hot flash when I think of Heathcliff and Rhett, and let's not forget Bogie. But, can we just pause for a spell? Can we reflect? If you recall, nothing worked out for these guys and the women who loved them. Nobody walked into the sunset holding hands."

Annie stared thoughtfully at Marge. After a while she said, "I know. I understand what you're saying. It makes sense. Love doesn't look so good when it's stacked up against life's opportunities."

"No, it doesn't," Marge agreed. "You give me hope, Annie. Maybe you haven't lost your marbles, after all." She drew in a breath and continued. "The foundation wants an answer, a written acceptance of their terms and conditions, Annie. We're talking about a great honor and a lot of money—not to mention a brilliant future.

But the decision's got to be made right away—by tomorrow.''

"I'll let you know," Annie said. "I need time to think." Both women had tears in their eyes when they hugged. "Thanks so much, so very much, Marge."

"I would have given twenty years of my life, Annie, to have offered to me what you have in the palm of your hand.''

"I know," Annie said. "But last night I was holding Chris. And—"

"Just think about it," Marge said. "Think hard, Annie. This is your whole life we're talking about."

Outside the gallery Annie found the afternoon traffic bumper to bumper. Radios sounded over engines, bicyclists whizzed by in bathing trunks and Day-Glo colored helmets, and roller-skating girls in bikinis drew male eyes from their sockets as they executed spins and sensual serpentine turns. Intermingling with the mechanized racket of brakes and gear-shifting, were gay human voices and the cry of a flock of gulls heading for the open sea.

And Annie loved all of it—right down to the exhaust fumes from a passing diesel Mercedes-Benz.

She had left Muffin asleep in the van, the windows open for air. August was just around the corner, and the sun was bearing down with serious intensity that afternoon. When Annie opened the Volkswagen's door, Muffin raised her head and blinked.

"Hi, Muff," she said, sliding into her driver's seat. "Major news flash: seems we can become rich and famous. No fuss, no muss. Or, we can stay here and find love and happiness. How does that grab you?''

Muffin stretched, then slunk out of her box, gave a hop and landed in the front seat beside Annie. She sat there like a true passenger, waiting for them to go forward.

"Where?" Annie asked. "Where to go?"

Muffin turned yellow eyes up to her, and with authority mewed the answer. Unfortunately it was in a language secret to cats.

Chapter Twelve

The next day the story of the canyon murder broke in the newspapers. The department had managed to keep a lid on it for the past several days while they pieced together whatever they could of the facts surrounding the case. The silence had enabled them to keep the curiosity seekers out of the area.

It was Chris himself who insisted the public had a right to know about the murder. If there was some nut out there on the loose, then people should have the opportunity to make intelligent decisions to protect themselves. Maybe that decision could mean nothing more than putting off a picnic in a remote canyon area. But it could save a life or two or three.

So on Wednesday the public was served some more bad news on a front page that already contained bad tidings of an environmental disaster and senseless fighting in the world's hot spots. But there was something about a local murder that brought the insanity down to where people could get a grip on reality.

Chris hoped that Annie might be shocked awake to her own very serious reality when she saw the paper he brought with him to her house.

He knocked on her door at ten in the morning. Her van was still outside, so he was certain she was home. He had to knock two or three times before she appeared.

She didn't look herself—that was the first thing he noticed as she stepped back to let him enter the house.

"Hi," he said, trying to get a fix on what was going on with her, but knowing better than to be too intrusive. "Looks like I came at a bad time."

She was wearing a robe still—unusual for Annie, who was always up and dressed before eight. Her eyes, usually glowing with light, were a dark, opaque blue, and there were uncustomary circles beneath her eyes. But even so she was beautiful, and he couldn't help but catch his breath.

Facing her, he remembered the feel of her body beneath his. But the attraction was more than merely physical. That his feelings for her ran far deeper than male lust was his cross to bear. It would have been so much easier for him if she had been merely a beautiful face with a body to match and nothing more.

Her manner was shy, the voice low when she responded, saying, "I guess I overslept." She glanced toward the newspaper in his hand, then looked up to his face again. "That's about the murder?" she asked.

Chris nodded. "I thought you'd be interested."

"I'd rather you had brought candy," she said dryly, and turned her back to him as she moved toward the kitchen. "I'm fixing coffee. Join me?"

"Thanks, no. I've had my quota for the day."

He followed her into the kitchen, where he leaned against a counter as she went about her mundane activities. The robe was loose. He saw the rise of her breast, the skin a honey gold as the material parted. She was unclothed beneath the robe.

Swallowing, he looked away as he fought against the urge to make love to her right there. He would open the sash, free her body and take her against the counter, there, now, with the sunlight tangled in her hair, dappling her body as he possessed her again and again, and . . . he was nuts!

He had come for a purpose that had nothing to do with lovemaking. Murder was the farthest thing from love. And the thought of his true mission that morning cooled his ardor immediately.

When she had made herself a cup of instant coffee, Annie turned to find the newspaper spread on the table. She hesitated, stiffening her shoulders.

When she looked up at him, he said, "Read it, Annie. It's why I came."

"Really? I never would have guessed, Chris," she said sarcastically.

She sank into her chair, and after taking one sip of her coffee, set the mug down and did not pick it up again as her eyes traveled from word to word, and line to line.

All the while, she felt Chris's eyes on her, watching, wondering.

The victim was the son of a man who had died the previous year of a heart attack. The murdered man had never owned much, and when he had inherited the ranch house, he had begun to make improvements. In order to afford the cost of his alterations, he had advertised for a roommate to provide extra income. The last roommate was a man named Kent Williams. Nothing was known of Williams except that he worked as a laborer in the building industry. Generally he would be classified as another transient passing through Southern California. Kent Williams had disappeared on the day of the murder.

On the day she had been at the canyon.

She lowered the paper to the table, staring at the bold captions over the story she had just read. Across the table Chris watched her, waiting for her to tell him what she couldn't.

She reached for her coffee, only to spill it.

Shaking her head at her own clumsiness, she pushed herself from the table and started for the sink to get a sponge. She never got there.

Chris caught her from behind, and turning her into him, kissed her hard. "Tell me," he said, releasing her just enough so that she could breathe. "Tell me what's hurting you, Annie. What's frightening you?"

"Nothing," she said. "Nothing."

But he continued as if she hadn't spoken. "I want to help. I can make things better for you, if you'd just let me."

Beneath his loving gaze she began to drink, feeling herself becoming stronger with each passing second. "Okay," she said. "I'll try."

Chris moved slowly around to his side of the table, watching her the entire time. Sitting, he said, "Don't worry. Whatever it is, I'll fix it for you—whatever it is, Annie, I'm going to make it okay. Tell me anything you can remember."

She nodded, then cast her eyes down to the newspaper again. Her hand trembled as she raised it slightly and began to read.

Fragments of that day in the canyon returned to her, but the memory of what actually had happened eluded her time and time again. It wasn't much that Chris was asking of her—only to remember what she had seen. Something stirred at the surface of her mind, a memory she could almost, but not quite, grasp.

With a whispery sob she let the paper fall, and anguished, said, "I *can't*. Nothing comes to me...nothing clear. I want to, but I can't remember." And she closed her eyes tight against her failure.

Chris placed his hand over hers. He understood. For some reason she had been forced to suppress what she had seen that day. Something had either happened to her, or she had seen something, and whatever it was was too painful or frightening for her conscience to acknowledge. If only she would trust him. If only she could understand that he would never in a million years let any harm come to her.

"It's okay," Chris soothed. "Sometimes people get blocks. They see something, or something happens that scares them and they just freeze up. It happens lots of times, and there are ways around it."

Annie's blue eyes, looking childlike with hope, were turned on him again. "How?" she asked almost eagerly.

"Different ways. Sometimes one single memory can trigger a complete release. Other times, there's hypnosis. But we've got to be careful with that, not that it's dangerous, but to use it as evidence isn't allowable in court except under certain conditions."

Annie listened attentively as Chris began to go over the evidence. "I'm going to tell you some extra things—things that weren't stated in the paper, but that might mean something to you."

Annie nodded.

"There were two sets of tire tracks besides the marks made by the victim's own car, and we narrowed the time—"

"What?"

Chris stopped. "The time was—"

"No, before that . . ." Annie's eyes were wide.

"I said there were two sets of tire tracks. . . ."

Annie closed her eyes. A tear slipped from beneath the dark lashes, followed instantly by two more. Chris rose and moved to her. "Hey . . . what is it?" Lifting her up, he brought her into his arms, stroking her hair, letting her lean into him. "Annie, tell me. What is it? Did you see something?"

"I don't know," she said. "I felt something—something sad and terrible. But I can't remember anything." Tears streamed down her face.

She was telling him the truth, and yet she wasn't. Not all of it, anyway. She remembered having seen something, something that frightened her that day, something that had made her run back to her van. But fear had obliterated her memory.

She looked to Chris like a tiny, frightened child, and he hated himself for having to be her tormentor. But he had no choice. He had a job to do, and her life might depend on him to do it right.

"I've got to make an official report, Annie. I've got to put you down as a possible witness."

"Why?" she asked. "I can't remember anything."

"It doesn't matter. You were there. The time you painted the scene, judging by the placement of the shadows in your painting, matches the time of the murder. Hal and Liz both know you were there that day, and I can't ask them to lie about it. And there's also no way I can be sure they haven't told any of their friends. Lies always unravel."

"Then I don't have any choice, do I? I'm officially a . . . a what? A suspect? A witness?"

"Technically, everyone's a suspect. But you're no killer. We'll leave it at witness." He looked at Annie, considering. Then he said, "What if we did call in a hypnotist? What if we don't touch on what you saw that day at all, but just play around—relax your mind, that sort of thing. There's a possibility that you could loosen up and—"

"No! Absolutely not," she said sharply. Her face had gone chalk white.

Her vehemence startled Chris. For an instant he was too stunned to say anything. "Why?" he asked. "What is it you don't want to remember?"

She turned away. "I don't want to submit to hypnosis," she said.

"But if you don't help me in this, there's a good chance that your life could be in danger, Annie. What you don't know—what *we* don't know—could hurt you," he finished, his tone sober.

"I've given you my statement. That's all I know," she said stoically.

"You mean that's all you want to know."

They stared at each other, equally matched in resolve to have his or her own way.

"Okay," he said, "I'm going to be straight with you. There's something really wrong here, Annie. I've said it before, and I'm saying it again. I don't entirely buy your stories of being a free-spirited gypsy artist. I don't buy the story that you don't know who fixed your wheel. Whenever I get into the past, you go hyper. Now there's this incident in the canyon, and you say you can't remember anything about that either. You've got a real problem and you don't seem to want to do much about it.''

"I do," she said, almost pleading. "It's just that—" But she broke off.

"Again? Again, Annie. You start, and then you just cut me off, cut me out. I love you, and you don't trust me.''

"I love you, too. Oh, Chris...I do." Her eyes were wide and wet with tears.

She looked delicate and fearful and feminine, and he took a step toward her, meaning to comfort her, and then stopped and shook his head. He suddenly saw that making it easy on her wasn't going to help.

"Somehow I'm beginning to doubt that," he said coldly. He made as if to leave.

"No, Chris!" Annie rushed toward him.

But he pushed her away. It was the hardest thing he had ever done.

He could still see her sorrowful stare as he turned from her and started out of the kitchen, saying without looking back, "I can't stay in love with a woman who can't trust me, Annie. That's not any kind of love."

He kept going, forcing himself to step through the door leading to the outside world with its killers and madness and unanswered questions. And for all he knew, he was stepping out of Annie's life.

* * *

Annie sat in her robe in the kitchen, looking down at the paper with its account of the canyon murder. She didn't know how long she was staring at the paper. Reality overwhelmed her now that she knew what she had to do.

There was no sense in trying to remember every detail as Chris wanted her to do. If she were meant to live through things again, then those things wouldn't have been kept from her. There were reasons the blackness came.

She loved Chris. She knew he loved her. But together or singularly, they were still no match for the past.

The phone rang. She let it ring. Then there was silence. Five minutes later it rang again. She was testing herself, firming her resolve to not jump to the world's dictates. She would have to toughen up. She was going to have to go on alone.

In ten minutes the phone pierced her thoughts for the third time, and stronger, she rose and answered its call.

"What did you decide?" Marge asked bluntly.

There was a long silence.

Annie looked beyond the window to where the ocean lay blue and eternal and depthless. "Yes. The answer is yes to fame and fortune."

She put down the receiver.

And wept.

Chapter Thirteen

Annie took painstaking care in planning the painting.

For more than three hours she did no more than sit on the front porch and look at the view. Gradually the feelings and colors had formed a solid impression in her mind. Taking up her pencil, Annie worked quickly, as if in a trance, as she transferred the interior vision to a blank piece of thin sketch paper.

Once satisfied with the perspective and composition, she began work in earnest, using oils.

For the next four hours, she did not move from her easel, painting with such concentration that it was only when Muffin hopped onto her lap that she realized it was mid-afternoon.

Her empty stomach growled as she looked at her work, and she smiled. "I got it right," she whispered, stroking Muffin's coat. "It's the way I'm going to always remember our time here." And she bent her head, rubbing away her tears in the silky gray fur.

She raised her face. Memories of the days and nights she had spent in this town squeezed her heart.

It was never going to come again. A love like that which she had found with Chris happened only once in a lifetime, if it happened at all. So she had been blessed.

She put away her paints and carefully brought the canvas into the living room, where she placed it back on the easel to dry. Muffin had padded along beside her, obviously interested in her dinner, which was generally served in the early evening.

Annie looked down, taking the hint. "Okay, pumpkin, chow's on."

She had just started for the kitchen, when behind her Annie heard a noise.

Chris.

Her heart leaped, and she turned expectantly to where his form would be silhouetted against the screen door, the sun a soft halo around his dark shape.

But there was nothing there; nothing but disappointment and the stillness of a summer's late afternoon.

Why had she hoped? Of course he would not return. He couldn't. He had left her yesterday, knowing that their relationship was futile.

The silence that followed the moment of hope grew increasingly dense, enclosing Annie in its reality of loneliness as she viewed her latest painting.

There he was—in the canvas. And he would be there forever, leaning casually against the post supporting the porch overhang. Her talent had made him live, had captured the warm pulse of life. His dark hair was caught in a breeze, and the eyes were alight with his soul's radiant fire. Not quite smiling, he had just spoken, or was about to call to her now.

Behind him the city of Laguna lay at the ocean's edge. Red tile roofs of Mediterranean-style villas mixed with the ubiquitous rustic brown shingles and redwood siding, and orange and magenta and crimson bougainvillea appeared bright under the hot southern California sun.

And in the foreground the lone figure, his eyes directed back to her—the viewer, the artist, the one who loved him and who would leave him within three weeks. And in time she would claim her place in the international art world, just as Marge had predicted. She would paint other vistas in other places. And she would hear other men call her name with hoarse desire, but she would never be able to answer them in kind. All her passion would be locked within the figure of a lone man in an oil she had painted one afternoon in a small California town.

Annie turned and made her way into the kitchen.

Muffin had become frustrated by the wait, she supposed, because when she looked, the cat had disappeared to mark time in some other place.

At work, Chris went over the three murders, contemplating scraps of information assembled in the three manila folders. Now and then he would consult the computer for cross-referenced data related to different aspects of each case, trying to find a common linkage.

Every time a phone rang, he would look up, tense with anticipation that the call might be from Annie.

And each time he was wrong.

He had made his grandstand play yesterday, walking out on her. If anything was going to happen between them, it had to be her move. They both understood that clearly enough.

The minutes of the day ticked by like centuries. To turn a page, seemed, to him, a feat requiring Herculean strength.

He forced his mind back to the reports before him.

All three victims were men; none had any criminal records that would have linked their murders to underworld vendettas; none appeared to have had any aberrant sexual predilections; and all had their lives taken by bullets. One had been a respected partner in a land development company—Chris's own father-in-law's; the second victim had been a land appraiser for a banking organization; and the third man to lose his life was a ne'er-do-well, whose only good fortune had ended in misfortune. He had inherited the property on which he met his end from a relative who had died a natural death the year before.

There was only one suspect—the itinerant roommate who had disappeared, a man who couldn't have been connected to Hal's partner or to the appraiser.

It was Jeff Parker who brought the first glimpse of sunshine into Chris's day, when shortly after two o'clock he slapped a printed report down on Chris's desk.

"Those payroll lists of construction companies you had me check out."

Chris looked up, half annoyed at having a thought interrupted. "Yeah? What about them?"

"Good thing you did. Kent Williams was working for Haverstrom Construction. I checked with personnel, and he's not there anymore. And guess what? The last day anyone saw him was on the day of the murder. Jolly good show, what?"

"Damn good," said Chris thoughtfully. "Thanks, Jeff." Chris reached for his phone.

Jeff turned to leave, then stopped and said, "Oh— I've been checking around on the Starstream thing, too."

For a moment Chris forgot about the canyon murder. A vision of Annie intervened. "And?"

"And you're right. Everything points to that Bonner guy having rigged the accident. But there's nothing on him. He vanished. There was a kid, too. The daughter of the lead singers survived."

"What happened to her?"

"Another mystery. I'm working on it. It takes dealing with those social welfare agencies, and the bureaucrats either don't know—which means they've either lost their files or are just too lazy to check anything out—or they're paranoid, man." Jeff shook his head, his bristly flat-top gleaming beneath the lights. He must have been out in the sun, for his nose was red and peeling.

"The girl's grown now," he went on, "but you'd think she was still eight years old. It's like they're committed to protecting her. I could get the combination lock to Fort Knox easier than getting them to turn over a file. To get a court order I've got to have some reason besides nosiness. But, not to worry, my friend. Sly's a word that wasn't invented for nothing—and sly's my middle name. I will prevail."

"Thanks," Chris said. "I really mean it. Thanks."

"Oh, almost forgot. You and Annie are invited over for dinner tomorrow."

Chris looked back at his computer screen. "Sorry, not possible."

"Something *else* planned, huh?" Jeff grinned lecherously.

"Yeah," Chris lied, feeling sick inside. "Something else," he mumbled, and hoped he wasn't going to have to get into his personal life with Jeff again.

"Even hot-blooded Italians have to eat, Farrentino. But, okay, another time. Enjoy your orgy." And he went whistling off, leaving Chris to make his call to Hal.

Hal's tanned face grew dark with concern as Chris related what he knew of Kent Williams.

As he spoke, sunshine coming through one of the plate-glass windows played over the building contractor's silvered hair. For an instant Chris thought of an archangel. All Hal needed was a gown and some wings.

Chris finished his account, and for an instant neither of them said anything as Chris allowed Hal to digest the information.

"I can't believe it," Hal said at last. "A murderer. A killer. Working for *me*. My God, Chris...someone here could have been in danger. And no one even suspected."

"Like they say, you can't judge a book by its cover, and we both know it's easy enough for someone clever to fudge on personnel checks. But for now I need to know anything I can about him. I want him off the streets and out of commission so no one else around here gets hurt."

"You said he's gone now."

"I don't know that for sure. He's not working construction for you—that's all we know. If he's crazy, he might still be hanging out in town. He could be working for someone else, or not working. You never know how someone's mind works when they're unbalanced.

With all the tourists around, it would be a perfect place to stay lost—just another face in the crowd.''

"You've got to have bulletins out, that sort of thing.''

"Yeah, well, here's the rub. We've got forty-six cops. Forty-six cops are no match for the number of bodies going up and down our beaches and streets.''

Hal looked thoughtful. "You know I want to do everything I can to help you, Chris. You can have total access to our personnel files, and feel free to question anyone on my staff. You say he was working as a carpenter?''

"That's how it shows up.''

"I wish I had known.''

"How could you have? Like you told me, you don't really get involved with that part of the business anymore. I think it's called 'delegating authority.' Don't blame yourself.''

Hal sighed. "No. I guess not. But I still feel... Oh, I know it's stupid, but I feel responsible. I suppose if I had any idea of what he looked like, I'd go out there myself and hunt him down.''

"Then I'd be out of a job," Chris said.

Hal smiled. "Then you'd have one here.''

Chris stood up, and Hal followed suit. "How's Annie?'' Hal asked as they walked together toward the door.

Chris hesitated, accustomed to keeping his feelings to himself. But Hal was the closest thing he had to a father since his own had died fifteen years ago. It wouldn't be so bad to open up, he decided; maybe it would even help.

"Annie and I are...we're having a rough time of it," Chris confessed. Saying her name aloud to someone else actually made him feel better, as if he had not lost her entirely.

"Oh, well, I'm sorry to hear that," Hal said, glancing over to him. "Nothing serious, I hope. She's a beautiful woman. And talented."

They were almost at the door, when Chris stopped, suddenly needing to talk about her.

"I'm worried, Hal. Annie was at the canyon that day—the day of the murder."

"Yes…why, that's right. Now that I think of it, you mentioned it at dinner. She did a painting, you said."

"Which she destroyed."

"She claimed it wasn't up to her standards."

"Yeah, well I don't buy that. I *saw* it. It was incredible. Really good work."

"So you're saying…?"

"Okay, I'm not a psychologist, but I think I know why she destroyed it. While she was painting, she saw something that upset her. It upset her so much that she tried to kill the memory by hacking away at the painting, which was an association of whatever it was that she saw. Apparently, she blocked the whole thing out of her mind. She claims she doesn't know what happened. But she does. I'm sure of it. It's just suppressed. Every time she gets close to remembering, she goes into a state of panic."

Hal nodded, his face grave. "Then she was an eyewitness to a murder. That's what you think?"

"I don't know. She could have been. Even if she didn't actually see the murder, she could have seen something that could lead us to the killer. What I'm afraid of is that someone—maybe the killer—saw her."

"Then she could be in danger."

"Exactly."

"Then you've got to get that guy—Williams, Kent Williams."

"If I could get Annie to remember, it would be a big step in the right direction. I suggested hypnosis."

"Hypnosis? Does that stuff actually work?"

"Sometimes. It depends."

"Well, by all means then—"

"That's not so easy. She won't submit to a hypnosis session. She seems afraid. I don't know why, but that's the way it is. Annie's...she's different, Hal." He shook his head and shrugged. "Maybe that's why I love her. I love the woman so much, I feel like I'm going crazy being away from her." He stopped then, realizing what he had admitted.

There was a moment of silence.

Hal turned and walked back to his desk. He sat down and with his head bent, folded his hands and stared at them contemplatively.

Chris felt uncomfortable. "I'm sorry...I—"

"No," Hal said, "it's fine. Don't be sorry. Love's a wonderful gift. I know you loved Laura. It's a compliment to my daughter that things were so good with her that you dove into the fire a second time." And he smiled then, looking up. "Notice I said *fire*?"

Chris nodded and smiled back, too. "I caught that. And you're right. Fire's the word. Feels that way, exactly."

Before he closed the door, Hal called to him again.

"Chris—if there's anything I can do to help...with the case, you know. Going through our records here...or if you just want an ear. Personal or professional, you know I'm here for you."

"Thanks, Hal. I'll remember that. And it means a lot to me."

Annie pressed down the lever of the electric can opener. The container of cat food began to revolve. The appliance was her own; she took it with her wherever she and Muffin journeyed. The whirring sound was one of those homey, familiar ones that always soothed her and excited Muffin. The cat's ears must have been trained to the machine's sound for she came running when she heard it. It was a ritual that always delighted Annie.

But that afternoon was different: Muffin didn't respond to the possibility of a treat.

Annie finished opening the can and dished out Muffin's evening portion, noisily tapping the spoon against the dish, then placed the bowl on the floor.

Still no cat.

She was about to resort to a verbal invitation to dinner, when a crash came from just outside the kitchen door. The sound was loud and easy to identify as one of her planters hitting the floor of the small utility porch.

But rather than becoming upset, Annie brightened. It meant that Muffin had come bounding toward the kitchen on her way to her treat. After undergoing the critical operation, it was a good sign to witness the cat's sudden spurt of energy.

Annie opened the door. She was right about the pot, but wrong about Muffin.

There was no cat, only a single large and smashed clay pot. The plant now lay felled on the boards, its roots partially exposed.

Calling out, Annie waited for a moment, searching for some sign of the cat before giving up and going back into the kitchen.

And there, staring up at her, yellow eyes pensive and unblinking, was Muffin.

But, of course, Annie thought, an uncomfortable chill traveling up her back . . . Muffin had been inside with her.

She pivoted slowly, looking to the kitchen door, with its large screened window. Beyond the screen she could see the outdoors. Varying shades of green trees and bushes covered the hill behind the house. The sun had moved. Now the back of the house was cast in the deepening light of late afternoon. Trees swayed slightly, whispering in the breeze.

She forced herself to move across the room to the door and turn the lock—for whatever good that would do. A sharp blade or a strong fist could rip away the screen in one motion. For an instant she searched the thick foliage again, her eyes moving right and left, searching as she had so many other times in her life.

But this time it was different. This time, whoever it was that was out there could be a killer—just as Chris had warned.

And then her attention fell again on the broken pottery. On the ledge from where it had fallen were several other smaller pots containing herbs Annie had purchased at the grocery store.

There was only the mildest of breezes outside. A pot the size of the one on the floor would have withstood such a light wind. And if there had been a freak gust of enough strength to do damage to such a heavy planter, then any one of the other smaller pots would have certainly been victimized first.

But they were all intact on the ledge.

Annie backed away. Her body was cold with fear, and her thoughts spun in crazy circles. She wanted to run again, but there was nowhere to go anymore. In three weeks, yes...but now, no. She was obligated to stay. Marge was counting on her.

"You could be in danger, Annie...."

Chris had warned her.

And now it was true. Even Muffin was alarmed. Someone was out there. And this time it wasn't someone who wished her well.

Chris returned to the department at a quarter to five. Nothing had turned up of value at Hal's, even after he had spoken with the personnel manager and had interviewed some of the workers who had been on jobs with Williams. No one knew much about him. He kept to himself, did good work and seemed to be a typical drifter, having only appeared a couple of weeks ago.

Lots of people—male and female alike—found their way into Southern California during the summer months, picking up easy money during the height of the summer tourist season and taking construction jobs.

He found a message on his desk from Jeff, who said he was leaving early for a dentist appointment. There were other calls, too, but none from Annie.

Somehow, he had thought there would be.

She had to love him. He loved her. And besides, he had *felt* her love, hadn't he? Yes. But he had also felt her fear.

He had intended to work late, if for no other reason than to fill up the empty space in his life. But suddenly he was weary. He planned to grab a bite to eat, go home and try to get some sleep. In the morning, with a fresh attitude, he might make some headway on his cases.

He was out the door and into his car when he remembered he should have locked a file. When he returned, the staff secretary had just fished her keys from her purse and was rising to leave for the day.

"See you tomorrow, Barb," Chris called as they passed each other.

"See you," she returned. "Oh, Chris..."

Still moving forward, he only half turned.

"You just got a call—"

"I'll call them back tomorrow."

"It sounded serious—from a woman. Annie."

Chris spun around. "Annie? What did she say?"

"Not much...just that she wanted to speak with you. She sounded worried. I don't know...maybe even a little scared."

Annie came to the door in a navy blue cotton pull-over sweater and jeans. She seemed to shiver, holding her arms across her chest even though the night was warm.

Chris followed her into the living room.

"What's going on?" he asked pointedly as she lowered herself onto the couch, choosing the right corner to huddle against. He decided to stand, believing it gave him psychological leverage.

"Nothing."

"Well, you look like a scared rabbit. My secretary said you sounded worried. The word 'scared' came up, too."

She seemed to consider his statement. When she spoke, it was without looking at him. Her dark gaze seemed unable to settle on one spot. "I thought about what you said. Maybe it's a good idea—the hypnosis."

His every instinct told him there was something wrong with this sudden change in attitude. He had wanted her to call him, of course; but the situation he had fantasized in his mind had been entirely different. Her agreement was to have been based on a sudden admission that she loved him enough to forgo her strange attachment to privacy. She was to have delivered a speech in which she would proclaim that trust and openness was going to be the cornerstone of their relationship. He had even envisioned candlelight, flowers, and soft music.

Instead, her face was pale and she appeared to have retreated even further into herself than before. The only difference was that she had called him to help her.

"Why the sudden change of mind, Annie?"

"Isn't that what you wanted?" Annie said, looking up at him.

There was a slight creak of a floorboard just then; maybe the house settling. To Chris it was nothing unusual. But Annie jumped, her eyes darting to where the noise had originated near the kitchen. Chris followed her glance.

It was Muffin. Sphinxlike, the cat sat like an immobile sentry, watching them from the door's frame.

"I wanted you to be safe," he said, looking back to Annie. "And I wanted us to be closer. You're not being honest with me."

"I don't know what you mean."

"I don't either. But I know I'm right. I'll call you tomorrow, when I get things set up for the hypnosis session. It'll be a professional therapist, and everything will be strictly confidential. You don't have to worry— whatever you find out during your session will be up to you to disclose at your own discretion." He started away. "It's all up to you, Annie."

But he stopped suddenly. He hadn't noticed it when he came in, but now he saw the painting displayed on the easel. Moving closer, he studied it. Time stopped as he was drawn deep into the work's intensity. Even in the waning light from the living room window, the whole canvas shivered with an internal luminescence.

And the man, the figure staring back at him from the canvas, was himself as Annie envisioned him.

What she had managed to create was extraordinary. It was as if she had caught his soul in the paint, trapped his essence in each stroke of her brush. Behind his painted image, the painted city of Laguna Beach grew out of the ocean's mist. But nothing seemed a mere representation. With color and canvas and passion, she had created a three-dimensional world on a one-dimensional plane.

Only once before had he been in the presence of such unique artistry outside a museum, and that was when he had first viewed the Starstream painting. He knew artists could mimic, but to capture the same feeling was remarkable.

If he hadn't known Annie was the artist, he would have expected the signed name on the bottom of the canvas to be Canaan. As it happened, Annie's name had not yet been added.

He turned, expecting to find Annie still huddled on the sofa. Instead, she had risen and was looking at him from across the room. The space separating them had grown fuzzy in the deepening light.

"Remarkable," he said at last. "It's remarkable. I don't know what else to say. I don't have the words to be more specific. All I know is that you're an incredible talent. There's no doubt in my mind that you could set the world on fire."

"Stay," she said suddenly. She had not moved from her place, and if she hadn't said it again, Chris would have assumed that his mind was playing tricks on him. "Stay," he heard her say a second time. The dark blue eyes glittered with tears.

Chris took a breath, closed his eyes for a second. "If I do," he said, looking at her again, "it's got to be on my terms. You've got to let me into your life, not just your bed."

She nodded. "I know." Her voice was very soft. "I'm going to the hypnotist. I'm going to try, Chris. Will you stay tonight?"

Chris sighed. He backed away from her beauty. The painting was in front of him, and looking into it, he found the answer in his own face staring back at him from the canvas. Of course he would stay. He had to. He loved her.

The night fell like velvet over their bodies as they lay entwined in Annie's bed. They made love slowly, their movements soft and fluid and warm.

Outside the window the trees rustled in the breeze. Then the world fell into a hush. Pale moonlight filtered through the leaves of trees, its pearlescent rays landing on the sheets.

He moved her astride him, and the pearls danced across her breasts and stomach and thighs, and slipped through his fingers as he caressed her breasts with his palms and tasted her skin.

And then suddenly it was as if the light had entered her.

Chris moved slowly, yet insistently, his hips transforming the stream of light into tiny flames.

She shuddered, sighing, abandoning herself to the rhythm that led her, that drove her, that now lifted her higher toward the single white-hot point of light.

And beneath her, Chris's body was a hot, twisting flame.

He cried out her name, and she clasped his shoulders, feeling the power of his legs, the strength of his shoulders as she answered him again and yet again.

Sleep came easily for Chris, but not for Annie. Satisfied and weary, he dozed within moments. Annie lay with her head against his chest, feeling his moist skin turn dry again. He had laced the fingers of one hand in her hair, and with the other pressed the small of her back.

It felt right. Everything felt right when they were together, Annie thought.

But it wasn't—not really. She had let him into her body again, but just as he had feared, her mind had remained off-limits. It would be right between them only when she told him everything about herself.

The hypnosis would be a beginning.

Or an ending.

The moon had passed behind clouds, and the room fell into darkness. It was quiet outside now. The trees no longer moved. Inside, she heard Muffin padding softly across the floorboards, then a light thud sounded, and Annie saw the animal perched on the windowsill.

Muffin sat immobile, staring into the darkened woods behind the house.

And Annie had the terrible feeling again that someone was watching back.

She moved closer against Chris, gripping him hard.

He stirred, coming suddenly awake. "What?" he said.

"I love you," she whispered. That was all. She could not say any more.

Chapter Fourteen

Chris was already up when Annie opened her eyes. She heard him moving about in the kitchen. The sounds were comforting. She smiled, then fell back into a contented half sleep. A couple of minutes later he was in the bedroom, handing her a steaming cup of coffee as he mimicked the bugling sound of the military.

"Rise and shine!"

Laughing, Annie sat up and kissed him as he joined her on the bed.

The way he looked ...

She longed to touch him. He was a vision of masculinity: the dark uncombed hair, shining brown eyes. Yes ... she wanted him.

"What?" he asked with a small laugh.

Annie felt herself coloring. "I was just thinking ..."

"We could do more than think about it," he volunteered, which only made her blush all the more.

"How do you know what I was thinking?" she challenged. "It could have been about pot roast!"

"It could have been, but it wasn't. And I know, because I was thinking the exact same thing. You're beautiful," he said, and reached with his free hand to run his fingers over the side of her face. He then trailed hs hand lower, moving the sheet and exposing her bare breasts. She shivered beneath his touch. "And I could make love to you now, all day, all night, all my life," he said, and their eyes met and held.

"So could I," she whispered. "So could I." She had never been so happy as she was at that moment. "But you have to go to work . . . don't you?" she asked with the hope that she would be wrong.

"Unfortunately, yes," Chris said, and replaced the sheet over her body. "But there's time to talk for a while."

"Okay . . . talk," she ordered, feigning imperiousness. "Tell me about your friend Jeff Parker."

And he did. They spoke of Jeff and some of the other men on the force—there were four detectives in all. Basically, Chris said, the Laguna Beach police had the same structure as that of a police department in a large city.

They had exhausted several subjects and were halfway through their coffee when Chris mentioned the broken pottery.

When he had let Muffin out that morning, he had found the smashed container on the back porch.

"It's too bad," he said, glancing sideways at Annie. "It looked like a nice pot. I don't know anything about plants," he went on, "but somewhere or other I got the idea that you could stick them in water and they'd root. Maybe that's some old wives' tale. Anyway, the plant's in the kitchen. I put it in a pot with some water. And I swept the dirt off the porch.'' He paused and, not looking at her, said, ''How'd it happen?''

''I don't know,'' Annie said, and knew that wasn't the right answer the moment it was out. It was too reminiscent of other vague replies she had offered to other questions he had posed. Already his eyes were on her as he considered her response. She should have realized that he hadn't been making idle chitchat. That wasn't Chris's way.

''Maybe the wind,'' she said with her eyes lowered.

''The others were smaller. They didn't fall down,'' he said flatly.

It was clear why Hal Haverstrom wanted him to take over his company. If there was a thief of paper clips, Chris would be on to him in a minute.

''No. I guess not,'' Annie said. ''Maybe it was Muffin.'' Her hand had begun to shake slightly, the coffee in the cup sloshing back and forth.

Chris closed his hand over her wrist, steadying her.

''So you just decided—out of the blue—to change your mind about being hypnotized, right?''

''It was what you wanted.''

''Hell, Annie!'' He swung off the bed and placed his cup on the dresser with a hard thud. When he turned, his face was dark with anger. ''You're afraid. That's why you decided to go through with my suggestion. What happened here?''

''Nothing...I just—''

''Don't play around, Annie. Just don't.'' He strode back to her and, taking the cup from her hand, set it beside his. He looked down at her in frustration. ''You just don't want to get it, do you? Look, this is serious. You may have been a witness to a murder. Someone else may know that. And you may now be in danger yourself. You know that as well as I do. That's why you changed your mind about the hypnosis, and that's why you called the department and sounded afraid. That's even why you asked me to stay the night and clung to me like a scared kid. Give me a break, Annie. I'm not stupid. It's my business to notice little things—especially little things that don't add up." He stopped and, taking a deep breath, moved away.

"Okay," Annie admitted, looking to where he stood leaning against the wall. "You're right. I was afraid. I just didn't want to worry you. I don't know how the pot fell, but I know it wasn't Muffin who knocked it over, and I know it wasn't the wind." She paused. "I thought maybe there was someone out there."

"Do you have any idea who it might be? This someone?"

"No. And that's the truth."

He sent her a long look of appraisal, as if weighing whether to believe her. Then he said, "I want you to get out of here. I want you to move into my place. Bring your paints, bring your cat, everything you want. But you move in. And you don't tell anyone where you are."

"I'll be okay here," she said quickly.

"I won't be okay worrying about you, Annie."

"I'm used to being alone, Chris." She looked at him beseechingly.

"You can get used to company, too."

"I have never lived with a man." Her voice held panic.

Chris stared at her disbelievingly. "That's what you think, huh? That I'm just 'a man'?"

"No, of course not. But—"

"But what?"

"It's just that I don't like moving in and out of people's homes," she said, and realizing she had given more of herself away than she had meant, she suddenly fell silent.

But Chris had caught her uncustomary slip. He didn't say anything for a while, just looked at her. Then he smiled, and in a wry tone, said, "So you don't like setting down roots because it hurts every time you have to pack up and go. And that was part of your life, your mysterious unknown past that you refuse to talk about."

"I moved around when I was young—yes. And it was hard. I never felt like I belonged anywhere. But even so, it always hurt when I had to say goodbye. It's better not to get too close."

"You don't have to move around anymore," he said. "You can afford to get close, Annie."

"You don't know that," she said stubbornly, almost with defiance.

"Whatever happened in the past—that's finished. We're starting over. Both of us are starting over," he said quietly.

With a shock she realized she had forgotten entirely about his situation. The invitation he had extended to her had to have been hard on him, too. He had his own grief to leave behind, yet he was willing to take that step.

As frightened as she was of setting down roots, she was equally as frightened of whoever it was that was stalking her.

"What's it going to be, Annie?"

"Let's start over," she said, not sounding happy about the prospect.

Chris smiled, looking extremely happy at the prospect.

Marge called when Annie had all but finished packing.

"Hi, darling . . . more news. I thought about the Farbinger grant, thought about it until my brain got blisters. And I've decided not to publicize it until the night of the show. I'm going to have a whole slew of art critics here that night, and I want to double whammy them with your importance. How's that sound to you?"

"Fine . . . it sounds just fine," Annie said, and bit down on her lower lip. It wasn't fine at all. She had to talk to Marge, had to explain that she was going to try to work things out here in Laguna with Chris.

"I'm so excited, Annie. This is the biggest thing that's ever happened to me. To actually be able to launch a major talent. Annie, I'm not sleeping at night. I've so many plans for you—for us. This is just the beginning."

Things were becoming more complicated by the second. "Marge, we've got to talk about—"

"Oh—listen, got to run. Someone just came in for a second look at one of the bronze sculptures. I'll call you later—"

She hung up before Annie had time to tell her she would be at Chris's. But then she remembered she had promised Chris to keep her whereabouts absolutely confidential.

"Can't I even tell Marge?" she had protested.

"No," he said. "Not anyone."

"But Marge, Chris? Do you actually believe that Marge might have anything to do with trying to harm me?"

"No. But Marge might tell someone else."

"You're an incredibly suspicious man," she said, shaking her head.

"I'm a cop. You get that way after a while."

So it was just as well, Annie rationalized, that she hadn't mentioned anything to Marge about leaving the house to stay with Chris.

As she continued to pack up the rest of her things, she practiced the speech she would give Marge when they had to come to terms about the Farbinger grant. It wasn't going to be easy.

Then again, everything depended on what happened in hypnosis. If it went well, she could build a real life in Laguna with Chris.

If it didn't, then she'd have to head on out.

Chris had worked with Sandra Berkus in the past. She was a licensed clinical therapist with a Ph.D. She was also an excellent hypnotist. There was no doubt in Chris's mind that she would be perfect for Annie.

"I don't want you to touch on the murder with her," he said. "I think she's got other stuff that should come first—things from her childhood. I'm thinking if she can talk about her formative years, the rest will come to the surface. If she can recall the details surrounding the murder on her own and not through hypnotic suggestion, then whatever she says is admissible evidence."

Sandra understood. She said she would work with Annie the following day.

Chris was just about to reach for the phone to call Annie when a call came in.

It was Hal.

"Just calling to check about dinner on Thursday," Hal said. "Liz said you were supposed to get back to her about what you wanted on the menu. She said something about roast beef. She lives to feed you," Hal said with a laugh.

Chris's mind was far from roast beef. It was hard to concentrate on anything but Annie. He repositioned himself and sat straight in his chair in an effort to train his attention on Hal's conversation. "Roast beef..." he said, picking up what he could of the dialogue.

"Thursday," Hal prompted. "Maybe this is a bad time to call."

"Sorry. I'm working on something."

"The murder, you mean."

"Yeah, the murder."

"Anything new?"

"Not really. We've got Kent Williams targeted as the most likely suspect. Wherever he is."

"And Annie? How's she?"

This time Chris smiled. But the smile did not last long. He had to break the news to Hal and Liz sooner or later. He took the coward's way out and blurted it out over the telephone. "Annie's moving in today."

There was a long silence.

"I thought it was best," Chris said. "Under the circumstances." He had made a mistake doing it this way. He should have done it in person.

"What circumstances would those be?"

"For one thing I'm worried about her, Hal. About her safety."

"Her safety?"

"I think she's being watched by someone. There've been a few incidents, all unexplainable, but they're mysterious enough to cause concern."

"I see," said Hal. "Well, in that case I can understand why you'd want to keep an eye on her—"

"No...no, wait a minute. Hal—you said we could be honest. So, look...painful as this is, I've got to tell you, I *want* her with me. Sure, I'm worried about her. But sooner or later, I would have wanted to be with her, anyway. This way is just sooner, that's all."

There was more silence on the line, and then Hal said, "It takes a bit of getting used to. Things moving so quickly lately."

Hal sounded upset. Chris ran his fingers through his hair and sank back in his chair.

"Yeah, well, they were bound to. They didn't move at all for a long time."

"When will she be moving in with you?" Hal asked.

"Today. She's packing right now, if she isn't at my house already. She'll be safe at my place. No one will know she's there." Chris paused. "And, Hal, don't mention this to anyone. Not *anyone*," Chris emphasized. "Tell Liz, of course. But make sure she understands that Annie's life may depend on complete and total confidentiality."

"Of course. You don't have to worry about any leaks from us, Chris."

"And about Thursday dinner," Chris said. "I'd like to come—and bring Annie, too."

"She's welcome anytime," Hal said stiffly.

"Thanks. You said that before, and I took you at your word."

"Look," Hal said, "Chris...this business about Annie moving in, I'm sorry if I sound a little upset—"

"No problem. I understand."

"Like I said, it'll take a little getting used to. It was where—"

"I know. It was Laura's house. Hal—I know this may sound really weird, but I know Laura would be happy for me. I don't feel any guilt. Not anymore."

"I guess it's a little harder for us. We don't have anyone to replace her with." There was a pause. "Sorry, Chris. That didn't come out right."

"Forget it. I know what you meant."

"Take care of her, Chris. We couldn't do anything to help Laura. But this is different. Take care of Annie."

"I plan to." Nothing was going to touch Annie's life from now on but good things, Chris vowed to himself as he dropped the receiver back into its cradle. She was under his care now.

Annie called Chris just before she left.

"Okay," she said, "I'm leaving now."

"What?"

"Going to your place," Annie said. "What did you think I meant?"

"I don't know. I just…hell, Annie. I'm as jumpy as a cat on a hot tin roof. You said 'leaving' and—Annie, I love you," Chris said softly, as if there were people around.

"Me too." She was smiling, but she wiped unshed tears away with the back of her hand.

"You didn't tell anyone you were going to my place?"

"No."

"Okay. Call me when you get there, just so I'll know."

She took a last look around the place, making sure she had secured the windows and the back door before leaving through the front.

She had already loaded most of her stuff into the van and had only her suitcase and Muffin in tow, when she began the final trip down to the street where the van was parked.

It was just past one, and the sun was hot, but the humidity was worse. The heavy air gave her the feeling that she was bearing the weight of the world.

Even the bees were not immune to the effect of the weather. Their buzzing sounded peevish and they circled around her furiously as she made her way down the walkway bounded on either side by the high, bushy oleander shrubs.

One large winged curmudgeon flew directly into her face, and though she knew that hitting a bee was an unwise thing to do, she nevertheless closed her eyes, raised her hand and swatted.

Her hand never came down. And when she opened her eyes, the world turned into a blur.

She was being swung to the side, forced off balance by whoever had grabbed her by the arm. The hold on her was strong and not sparing of pain. She could hardly breathe—fear mixed with the dense air, cutting off her supply of oxygen.

When she tried to scream, nothing came out. She tried again, but this time a hand was clamped over her mouth, and she felt something hard and cold being pressed against her temple. She was dragged to the side, where a cluster of bushes cut off the path's view from the street.

She had dropped her suitcase, and now as she struggled to gain her freedom, she tripped over it, sending her attacker off balance along with her.

It was then that she saw the gun, dull black with a long cylindrical attachment. She saw it, airborne, as it passed by her. And she, too, was being flung to the side.

Her head hit the cement terracing. Then there was nothing.

Chris called his home number at least ten times, waiting for Annie to pick up the phone. He called Annie's number another ten times. Then he called Marge Briskin at the gallery, thinking that Annie might have stopped there before going to his place.

In between calls, he had police business to handle, but he did it badly. His mind was on Annie. She should have called him by now. She should have been at his house by now.

He was in the middle of a call to the bank manager who had worked with the murdered bank appraiser, when Jeff Parker stood in front of his desk, looking down with a troubled face.

Chris ended his call immediately.

"What?" he asked.

"Take it easy now," Jeff said, but even he did not look very calm.

"Take what easy?" Chris wanted to know. He had already risen slightly in his chair, as if expecting to be called upon to bolt to the scene of some heinous crime.

"Annie's been attacked—"

Chris jumped to his feet. "Where is she? How bad is it?" His hand was on his revolver, as if called to a duel.

"I don't know. The call just came in over dispatch. An ambulance and police vehicle are on the way."

And so was Chris.

Chris tried to remain calm in Annie's presence.

It was almost impossible. It was the first time he had been in a hospital since Laura had died, and now, to see Annie lying in bed, her head bandaged, was hard for him to bear.

"You're safe now," he said, sitting beside her bed and holding her hand tightly in his. Her hands were scratched, a red antiseptic paint making the damage look worse than it probably was. "No one can hurt you anymore," he repeated, as much for his own peace of mind as for hers. But of course, that's what he had promised her before. He had let her down.

The only good news was that the man who had attacked her was in police custody. All she had to do was to identify him as her assailant.

"Do you think you could recognize him in a police lineup?" Chris asked, speaking softly and with a surprising calm he certainly did not feel.

"I didn't see him," Annie whispered back, her voice weak, her expression bewildered.

Her fragility only served to increase Chris's rage. "What do you remember? Maybe if you start with small details, then you'll remember—"

"No. I never saw him. He came from behind. It all happened so fast."

"Annie, listen...we've got the guy. He's in lock-up right now, down at the station. But we can't hold him unless we can get something concrete on him."

"How did you catch him?" she asked.

"You won't believe it," Chris said. "He called the police."

"But...why?" Annie asked, her blue eyes clouding with more confusion.

"Search me. Maybe he's nuts. He claims he saved you from someone else." Chris reached for the manila folder at the side of his chair, and slowly began to remove a photograph. "I've got this snapshot of him."

Annie turned her head to the side, as if revolted.

"Annie, I know you've been through a lot. But if you can just take a look...just see if you recognize him."

"Oh, Chris... I don't want to think about it anymore. I just want to be free of all the awfulness."

"Annie, so do I. I want it for you, and I want it for us. But if this guy's dangerous, we've got to put him out of commission. He could be some itinerant, or he could have something to do with the murder."

Annie nodded. "Okay. Show me."

Annie accepted the photograph. Her face went white and took on the expression of a hunted animal. Lurching up in the hospital bed, she flung the photograph to the side. "No!" she screamed. "No! No!"

Chris grabbed hold of her and held her while she sobbed against his chest. "You're okay, baby... you're okay. That's all we needed. I'm not going to let anyone hurt you again."

She fell back against the pillows, appearing drained.

"You recognized him. He's the one who attacked you. And maybe the one at the canyon?" Chris pressed.

"He's the man who killed my family," Annie said dully.

"What?"

"It's Corrie Bonner. He's changed... but it's Corrie." And her eyes filled with tears again.

She told Chris her story, about being afraid all the years, but not wanting to deal with her fears. She knew that people thought Corrie Bonner might come after her, might try to kill her. But she didn't want to believe that. As a child she had liked Corrie. She'd lost everyone and everything: she didn't want to lose her good memories of Corrie, too. In her mind she had always pretended the crash had been an accident.

"My God," Chris whispered, when she had finished her tale. "You're Canaan."

Annie explained about the necessity of changing her name.

Chris listened, all the pieces suddenly fitting together.

For years, Bonner had been stalking Annie. He must have followed her to Laguna Beach. Why he hadn't killed her before, or even that day, was anyone's guess. Perhaps, Chris thought, Bonner had held on to Annie because she reminded him of Michelle, Annie's mother, the woman he had loved. Killing the entire Starstream group was the act of a madman; any motive Bonner had didn't necessarily have to follow logic.

And, Chris considered further, if he was lucky, Bonner—using the name Kent Williams—was also the man who had committed one canyon murder. If he was to be even luckier, Bonner would finally be put away. And Annie, and a lot of other people, would be safe from the psycho.

But for the time being, Chris had to act fast, or Bonner would be out on the streets again. Without Annie to identify him as her attacker, which she could not do, they could not hold him. Bonner had called the police and the ambulance, which was, in fact, the act of a Good Samaritan. There were no prints on the gun.

Even if they picked him up on the long-outstanding warrant, a lawyer could get him bail easily. There was nothing on him, really, but supposition and circumstantial evidence.

From what Chris understood from the cops who had taken Bonner into custody, he claimed to have saved Annie's life by interrupting an attack by another man. Chris told the officer who relayed the information that he believed that as much as he believed the moon was made of Swiss cheese. Bonner was just a crazy, lying scumbag criminal. All Chris could think of at the time was Annie, of protecting her from Bonner and every other possible harm.

Lying against the sheets, Annie was almost as pale as the linen. He stood up and kissed her lightly on the lips. "I'm going to let you get some rest now."

"Chris . . . !"

He turned back.

"I'm afraid."

"Annie—the guy's locked up. You're safe now."

"But what about later? Chris? I want to do the hypnosis."

"We will. I've set it all up, and when you're back on your feet, we'll—"

"No. Now. Now, Chris.

"Really?"

"I want to."

Sandra Berkus had the perfect kind of looks for a therapist. Everything about her inspired confidence. Her eyes were a soft, warm brown and her hair a light, shining, straw blond worn in a smooth pageboy. And when she spoke—"Ten, nine, eight . . . you are getting more relaxed. . . seven, six. . . ever more comfortable and relaxed"—her voice soothed.

Then the years floated past Annie until she returned to her eighth year.

"What happened when you were eight?" Sandra asked. "Can you remember anything important?"

"Yes," Annie said. She breathed deeply, the pictures coming into focus.

"Tell me what you see," encouraged Sandra.

"Fight. A fight," Annie said, her voice small, like a child's.

"What's happening in the fight?"

"My mother and father, having a big fight. Corrie there, too. My mother says she is going to leave. My father is angry. Says he is going to kill her. If she leaves him, he is going to kill her. He says he will kill me, too." Annie's voice had become very small, and then she was still.

When she awoke, Sandra held her hand and told her that she did very well. "How do you feel?" she asked Annie.

Annie thought for a moment. "Sad," she said. "Seeing them again."

"Do you feel any freer?"

"A little, yes. All those years of not wanting to think about what happened that night. It was so ugly. I guess it must have hurt too much, thinking that my father would try to kill my mother, and that he would kill me, too. My own father," Annie said sadly, and shook her head.

"He wasn't thinking right, Annie. I'm sure he loved you."

"He was obsessed," Annie said. "He was crazy."

Chris was waiting for her after the session. He came into the hospital room after Sandra left and asked Annie how it went. She told him, and he listened raptly, trying to fit the pieces of the puzzle together.

"I'll be back later," he said, appearing to Annie in a fog. "I've got some checking to do, and you've got some dreaming to catch up on." He bent down to where she lay propped against her pillows, and kissed her. When he started to pull away, she wrapped her arm around his neck and pulled him back.

"I love you," she whispered into his ear. "I love you so much."

"Annie...this is all going to be over soon. I promise," Chris said.

"Chris?" Annie called as he was almost out the door. "There's something else. It was Corrie Bonner I saw at the canyon."

Chris froze, almost afraid to hope for such good news. "You're sure?"

"Positive."

Chris nodded. "Good girl," he said. "Good girl."

"I don't feel very good," Annie said. "I feel awful. It just seems wrong."

"Murder's always wrong," Chris said.

"No—something else. Something's wrong." Weary, she closed her eyes, and within seconds drifted off to sleep.

With Jeff working alongside him, they managed to trace the couple who had watched Annie for Michelle on the eve of the accident. What he discovered during his conversation was startling.

"I never told no one this," the woman said. "Thought it might hurt Canaan...or Annie—I guess is what people call her now. But it's been so long. Maybe now's the right time. It'll be okay to talk about it."

"What's that?" Chris asked, pressing the telephone closer against his ear.

"Rod Palance wasn't Annie's father. It was Corrie. Corrie Bonner was Annie's real dad. That was Michelle's big secret. She'd always loved Corrie, but you know how things happen sometimes with love."

"Yeah," Chris said. "I guess I do."

"Well, things got twisted and confused for a while between Corrie and Michelle, and she ended up marrying Rod. Then she was sorry, and every time she tried to leave Rod, there'd be a lot of bad stuff—violence, threats. Michelle was too afraid. So Corrie stayed on with the band to protect Michelle and Annie. Finally they were going to make a break and leave together. When Rod found out, he went crazy and told Michelle he was going to kill them. Michelle left Annie—Canaan, then, with us. Later, Michelle was going to make a run for it, once she knew that Annie was safe. Corrie was supposed to come by our place and get Annie. So you get it? Later, Michelle was going to sneak off and join them."

But of course, Chris reasoned, it never happened that way. The accident occurred and Corrie became the prime suspect, a hunted man whose only recourse was to watch over Annie from afar. After Michelle had died, all his ambition had gone with her. Annie was all he had left in life. It was for her that he lived. Corrie had been Annie's guardian angel all those years—afraid to come forward for fear he would be put away and then Annie would be left totally unprotected.

A new scenario of the Starstream crash formed in Chris's mind.

It wasn't Bonner who had rigged the accident: it was Rod Palance. Rod had killed Michelle, who he knew he'd lose to Bonner, anyway. And, in doing so, he knew he could blame the whole thing on Bonner. If he couldn't have Michelle and Annie, Rod didn't want to live.

On the other hand, Corrie Bonner was still the man Annie had witnessed at the scene of the canyon murder.

Oh, God, Chris thought, staring at the face of his computer. Annie had thought she was identifying a

murderer. What was it going to do to her when she
learned that the man she was condemning was in actuality her real father?

It was during the late evening visiting hours when
Chris came to her bedside with a bouquet of red roses
in a vase.

"They're beautiful," she said, smelling them. She
smiled up at him, looking sweet, even with the white
bandage wrapped around her head.

"You're beautiful," Chris returned, and took the
roses to a dresser. When he turned back, she was still
smiling.

"Annie, I'm sorry, but you've got to know something..."

And when he had finished, she was no longer smiling.

"I can't believe it," she said. Her voice was a mono-
tone.

"Of course you can't."

"My father...Corrie Bonner? A murderer?"

"He's probably sick, Annie. His head isn't good
anymore. He's had a lot of hard knocks in life."

"And now he's going to have the hardest of all," she
murmured. "Because his own daughter is going to be
the one to pound the last nail into his coffin."

"He did it to himself, Annie."

"Chris," she cried out, her eyes pleading, "he's my
father. And even if he's crazy, he meant me no harm.
He spent his life following me around just to make me
safe. And now I'm going to destroy him!"

"You don't have any choice. I don't have any choice.
It's the law." Saying it sounded so cold to Chris. But
there it was. There had been more than one occasion

during his term on the force when he had been confronted with moral dilemmas of his own. But he couldn't rewrite the laws according to his own whims. That's why it was the law.

"I feel like I ought to see him."

"He's in the county jail now. We can only keep prisoners overnight."

"I feel like I should, but I can't. Chris... it's too confusing. I don't know who he is. I don't know if he's good or bad or crazy, or what."

"He's probably a little of everything. We all are to some extent."

The following morning, when Chris came by to see Annie at ten, she was dressed in her street clothes, still with the white bandage wrapped around her head.

"What's this?" Chris asked, laughing.

"This is the woman you're taking home with you," she said, and grimaced. "Finally."

Chapter Fifteen

Annie sat beside Chris, her head bandaged in white gauze and the dim traces of Betadine still evident on her arms.

But bumps and bruises were unimportant when contrasted with her inner contentment as Chris navigated the car through the traffic on Pacific Coast Highway, past all the now-familiar Laguna Beach landmarks.

This was *her* town now, *her* place, and next to her sat *her* love.

"I'm happy, so happy," she announced buoyantly, her voice clear despite the traffic's roar.

Chris smiled, looked over to her and reached for her hand. He squeezed her fingers gently. "And I promise it's only going to get better and better from now on."

"I know," she replied with the same conviction. "I know." For a while the more sober aspects of her life were forgotten.

"Sorry, but I've got to run as soon as I get you settled in," Chris said, interrupting her happy musings. "Wish I could stay, but—"

"Oh, no. Oh, Chris... I thought we'd have the morning. Couldn't you find a way?" Annie asked hopefully. Beneath the white bandage her soft brown hair created a frame around the delicate oval of her face.

With a slight smile and a caress of his brown eyes, Chris brushed away a bothersome lock that the wind whipped across her cheek.

But the smile waned into a look of resolve, and Chris sighed and shook his head, directing his attention back to the road. "You know I want to. But there's stuff that can't be put off."

With the last sentence, Annie noted that his tone had grown ominous.

"You mean stuff about my attack." Annie looked beyond the window. The scenery suddenly appeared to her less lustrous than it had a moment before.

"That—and the canyon murder."

"You're convinced they're connected, aren't you?"

Chris changed lanes behind a slow-moving truck, then dodged back into the fast lane. "Perhaps highly suspicious is more correct."

"But you really think that Corrie Bonner was responsible for both incidents. And that's what you're going to try to prove."

"Let's just say it would make things a whole lot simpler all the way around if he were."

"So you could close your case."

"That would be nice, yes. I'd get a few pats on the back and maybe a day off to go fishing. But more important, you'd be safe."

"He's my father, Chris. My *father*," Annie emphasized in exasperation.

Chris looked her way and reached for her chin. "Annie, look, I understand how you feel—"

She shook her head, liberating herself from his gentle touch. "No. You don't know. How could you? I didn't think I had anyone left in this world, and now I find out I have someone, and I'm expected to believe he tried to kill me? I'm supposed to believe he's a crazy man who wants me dead and who killed someone else for no reason? I can't accept that. I can't, Chris."

"No matter what you feel, or what I feel... the facts don't change."

"Chris, it's not just that he's my natural father—which I've got to tell you is something I'm having a hard enough time accepting—but I don't remember Corrie as being anything but kind and rational and totally sweet in every way. Corrie Bonner's not a killer. To me that's as much a fact as anything you've got on him so far."

"You were a kid, Annie. Kids don't always pick up on all the subtleties."

"Well, I disagree. I think kids pick up on everything. Except for that one night—when I heard the fight, the threats—my feelings for Corrie were completely positive. Which is why I must have blocked out the incident. The shock was just too much for me. For *her*," Annie amended. Then, more wistfully, she added, "Strange, but I don't think of myself as Canaan. It's almost as if she and I are separate people."

"Well, you were. For a long time."

"That's what Sandra Berkus said—that I had to be in order to survive emotionally."

Chris edged the car in to the left-hand turn lane and waited for the signal to turn yellow before negotiating the turn off the main highway. They had just cleared the center divider when Annie saw the car.

Her blood ran cold. She stiffened, then whipped her head around to catch a glimpse of the dark blue Ford with the sticker on its bumper. *Dart-Away-Rentals.*

For an instant she remembered standing at the side of the road as another dark blue Ford—same model, color, sticker on its chrome bumper—sped off the road leading from the canyon area and onto Laguna Canyon Road.

Her thoughts jumped back and forth from then to now, from now to then, and back to Pacific Coast Highway where she watched the blue Ford. Her eyes burned as she followed its progress down the highway's slope toward the center of town. The driver was different... hatless.

A hat.

Yes, yes. That was it: the driver she had seen speeding out of the canyon had been wearing a hat. A blue-and-yellow baseball cap, and it had... it had...

Annie squeezed her eyes shut in her effort to remember,

...a circle.

She felt Chris's hand on her arm, heard the concern in his voice. "Annie? What's going on? You're okay?"

She didn't answer, couldn't break the train of her thoughts. The images were coming now, fast and tentative. There was a circle on the hat with a number, and the number... it was a one. The number one.

The man wearing the cap had turned; just for an instant he had turned his head to the side, and that's when she had seen the number.

"Annie!"

Abruptly she found herself staring into Chris's alarmed brown eyes. "Chris...Chris...I remember," she said emphatically. Her eyes were wide with excitement as she described the scene she had recalled. "That day at the canyon, there was a blue Ford. It was dark blue, a new car—not an expensive model, but a rental. Dart-Away-Rentals, that was the sticker on the back bumper. I just saw another one exactly like it, and that's what made me remember. The man driving it on the day of the murder...the man was wearing a blue-and-yellow hat, like a baseball cap. It had a circle over the visor, and in the middle was a number one."

"What?" Chris interrupted suddenly, his brown eyes sparking. "What did you just say?"

"I said that there was a rental car and—"

"No, no..." he said impatiently, and slammed his palm down hard and flat against the steering wheel. "The hat. What about the hat?"

Annie repeated herself. She watched as Chris's eyes narrowed. Encouraged by his attentiveness, she rushed on. "Whoever was driving that car, Chris, was probably the killer. The guy who got killed was alive when Corrie—my father—left. Maybe it wasn't Corrie. Maybe it was this other guy who did it."

Instead of the gladness she had expected, Chris's expression lost its momentary alertness and assumed a heavy melancholy. He neither slowed nor accelerated, merely continued a steady course up the hill. His brown eyes, flat and dull, were trained on the road.

"Anyway, that's my theory," she said.

"Your theory..." Chris repeated.

"Okay, you don't believe me," Annie said with a tinge of annoyance that he wasn't showing any enthusiasm over her breakthrough revelation. "You think I've invented this to save Corrie, right?"

"Annie..." He said nothing more, and instead drifted back into his silence.

"I'm sure," she said stubbornly. "I'm sure of what I saw."

"You can't be responsible for another human being's actions."

"Why all the platitudes!" she exploded. "I'm giving you clues, evidence. Isn't that what you detectives want?"

"You're snatching at straws—"

"No. Okay, yes. Of course I don't want to have to be the one to send my own father to jail. But I know what I saw. I'm an artist, Chris. I notice things, details." She stopped suddenly. Looking at him, she said in an entirely different tone, "And I'm noticing that you don't want to believe me."

He didn't respond at once.

Finally he cleared his throat. "I look at facts, Annie. But they've got to be facts based on real evidence that can be substantiated in a court of law. I don't want you to get your hopes up, be disappointed and then blame me for not being able to change the truth. If Corrie Bonner's our man, then that's that."

"Fine. All I'm asking is that you check out what I've told you. Will you?"

Chris sighed heavily. "Sure," he said. "That's my job."

Once home, it took about a half-hour for Chris to arrange her on the living room sofa, surrounding her with enough pillows to satisfy a pasha's appetite for luxury. The arrangements also included a large tray heaped with food.

"Just in case you want to nibble," Chris claimed in total seriousness.

"Do you think I'm an army?" Annie asked with a bemused smile, looking up at him from amid her cloud of upholstered foam.

"Maybe I should get a couple of blankets," he suggested, ignoring her humor.

"It's summer, Chris. The temperature today will hit the high eighties, so I may melt, but I don't think I'll catch a chill."

He studied her then. His expression was both concerned and disbelieving. "You're sure?"

"Positive," she said with authority.

He laid a quilt on the end of the sofa anyway. "Just in case."

"You're crazy," she said, laughing.

"Yeah." He nodded solemnly, his brown eyes drinking her in. "I'm crazy in love with you." He bent to kiss her.

She twined her arm around his neck and was pulling him into her nest of pillows when loud knocking on the front door interrupted her seduction.

It was Hal. He stepped past Chris and into the living room. He was carrying a flat white box with a ribbon around it, and spoke in a rush. "Sorry to barge in, but Liz insisted I drop these cookies off on my way over to the boat. That Japanese consortium is joining me for lunch." He placed the box on a table. "Saw your car outside, or I would have just left them at the door. Anyway, they're chocolate, so it's just as well they're out of the heat." He turned back around to Chris.

A beam of sunlight illuminated Hal as if he were in a spotlight. He was dressed in a lightweight navy blue blazer with gold nautical buttons that gleamed like coins. Beneath the jacket was a white polo shirt with red buttons to match the belt. His slacks and Docksiders were a bright white. Annie imagined him on the hundred-foot motor yacht that Chris said Hal owned and kept docked in the Newport marina.

"Good God," Hal swore as he turned from Chris toward where Annie was nestled amid the pillows. His eyes widened as he took in the bandage circling her head. He stepped forward, as if in a trance.

"What on earth? What is this?" Hal demanded, outraged.

Before Chris could answer, Annie said, "It's okay. Really. I look much worse than I am."

Hal looked to Chris for assurance. "An accident? What happened?"

Chris gave a brief, matter-of-fact explanation, leaving out the details—and any emotional embellishments, which Annie found amusing. Men. They had to put on a show of indomitable strength in front of each other.

Hal's face turned a ghostly white. "That son of a bitch..." he growled. "My God, Chris...she could have been—"

"But she wasn't. And everything's going to be okay."

"He's locked up?" Hal snapped like the grand inquisitor.

"Yes," Chris responded evenly. "For the time being."

"What the hell does that mean?"

"It means that we can't hold him as Annie's attacker if she can't identify him. Tomorrow she's going to have a second session of hypnosis. Otherwise, all it'll take for the suspect to get out is a good lawyer and some bail money."

"Good God." Hal turned to Annie. His voice had lost none of its officiousness when he announced, "I'm hiring a bodyguard for you, young lady."

Annie protested. "Really, I don't think—"

Hal overrode her. "Okay, I'm going to be honest— brutally frank." He shifted his eyes from her to Chris, then back again. Behind the blue was a rage. "We lost our Laura, and the pain is beyond comprehension. Chris and Laura were our family. We were a small family, the four of us, but we were a real family. And then you came along, and I won't say it wasn't uncomfortable for us at first." Hal drew in a deep breath, and the fire behind his eyes dissipated somewhat as he exhaled. "But we've become fond of you, Annie. And we see that you will be a part of Chris's life from now on, so we're hoping that you'll include us in your lives just as we want to have you in ours. If anything happened to you—well, Liz and I, we could never live with it. So if not for yourself, then for us. And for Chris's peace of mind I hope you'll let me follow through with some round-the-clock protection until this matter's concluded and we can be certain you'll be safe."

Tears had come to Annie's eyes. She was about to express her gratitude for Hal's concern when Chris spoke first.

"She's safe here, Hal." Chris wedged himself between Annie and the imperious and commanding presence of his father-in-law. "Annie's safe with me."

The two men stared at each other; two strong, virile, determined men. Hal waited a beat, obviously taking the time to assess his position.

"Of course." The older man's voice was low and moderate; it was the tone of a seasoned negotiator. "I didn't mean to imply—"

Chris didn't allow him to present his case, instead taking control of the situation himself. "I understand you mean well. But Annie's under my care now, and nothing's going to harm her again."

By his dismissive tone and the ice blue of his eyes, Hal was not yet ready to assume his secondary position in the matter. "If I could be sure of that—"

"You can be," Chris said firmly.

A moment passed, then Hal nodded. "Fine. We're in agreement." Hal looked past Chris to Annie. "The issue is Annie's safety, and since we're in agreement there, the matter's closed." He smiled warmly and met Chris's eyes again. "I'm sorry if I came on a bit presumptuously, Chris. I guess it's second nature to want to take over, even when it's not my place."

"No problem," Chris said, and the tension in the room disintegrated into smiles and light conversation.

The phone rang. Chris picked it up, and spoke briefly. By the conversation Annie knew he was speaking with Jeff Parker. When Chris hung up, his eyes were clouded.

"Sorry," he said. "I've got to take off." He picked up his keys, then kissed Annie lightly on the forehead. "I'll call," Chris said, the look in his eyes telling her he loved her.

He turned to Hal.

"I'll walk you out," Chris suggested.

"Sure." Then reconsidering, Hal said, "On second thought, I'll put the cookies away so they don't melt." With a smile to Annie, he said, "You've got to try at least one so I can report back to Liz. You know how seriously she takes her cooking." He patted Chris on the back and saw him to the door.

Annie watched them, her heart warm. If there had been any dissension between the two men before, it had been erased by the deep affection that was so clearly evident now.

Chris backed out of the drive, his eyes trained on the rearview mirror. He was less interested in the driveway than the car parked out on the street.

But there it was. With dread he focused on the blue-and-yellow logo with the number one emblazoned in its center. Beneath it, in elegant black script read Haverstrom Company.

A sick feeling churned in Chris's stomach, and he looked away, disgusted with himself.

Hal couldn't be connected. It was impossible. What was he thinking of?

He remembered seeing the new logo in an artist's rendering. The drawing had been on Hal's desk then. And the moment Annie had mentioned the design, the drawing had come to mind. He hadn't known that there were also hats with the logo.

But a hat didn't mean much. Anyone could wear a hat.

The sickening feeling abated. By the time he had arrived at the Spanish-style building that housed the City Hall, the fire department and the police facilities, he had other things on his mind.

Jeff Parker was waiting for him at his desk. "How's Annie?" he asked.

"Okay. She's okay. So what do you have?"

Jeff pulled over a chair and ran down a list of possible suspects and motives in two cases unrelated to the canyon murder.

"Hey, Farrentino," Jeff said loudly. "You with me, or what?"

"Yeah, sure."

"You're a million miles away."

"What do you have on the canyon murder?"

"It's not the only case we've got going, Chris. There's other—"

"Damn it!" Chris slammed his fist on the desk top. "It's the only one with a nut who can kill the woman I love." His eyes locked with Jeff's. "Sorry," Chris muttered, and sank back into his chair.

"Okay," Jeff said. "I'll forget everything but the canyon killing. Where do we go?"

Chris gave him a list of clues to check out.

Jeff looked at him quizzically. "Are you kidding me?"

"I hope so. Just do it, okay?"

"Aye-aye, Captain," saluted Jeff, standing. They looked at each other for a moment, both searching for the right thing to say. But there wasn't anything, and Chris turned away, feeling half like a fool, half like a monster.

There were calls Chris had to make, and paperwork. He placed three calls, his thoughts unfocused as he struggled to keep up with the conversations, and finally gave in to complete inertia.

He sank into the chair and stared at the telephone. The dull throbbing in his temple had become a jackhammer's assault, and a sickening feeling began to squeeze his insides again.

Leaning forward, he gripped the receiver in his hand and dialed. The phone rang four times, five times. He was standing, his muscles straining as he tightened his fingers around the plastic handle.

On the sixth ring she answered.

"Hello?"

"Annie...Annie..." And he began to laugh.

"Chris...what...why are you laughing?" she asked, smiling in amusement.

"I—I thought...you took so long to answer... God, Annie...nothing. How're you doing?"

"Great. Except that I've eaten half the cookies. Chris, Hal's really wonderful. I feel so...I don't know...so full of love. For you...for everyone. Chris..." He could hear her crying. "I'm so lucky."

The sick feeling in the pit of his stomach began to ebb.

Chapter Sixteen

She had planned the evening carefully—the candles were lit and she had ordered pizza, which she had kept hot in the oven until Chris had come home. Tonight was going to be a fresh start. She wasn't going to have any more secrets in her life.

She knew he was going to be upset when she told him about the grant from the foundation, but after she finished her apologetic spiel, "devastated" was a more apt assessment of his mood.

He sat across the table, looking at her through the flickering glow of two candles. He said nothing, just stared at her, his handsome face splintered into a mosaic of grief.

"You were actually going to walk out on me? On us? On everything we had?" He was stunned. "Maybe we hadn't known each other a long time, but what we had was... It was so strong."

After a time she said, "I didn't understand what I now know. I thought it was my best alternative under all the circumstances. But the circumstances changed."

Suddenly, he rose from his chair and sent it skidding behind him as he stalked over to where she sat, frozen now in apprehension.

Grabbing her up from the chair, he took her by the shoulders and gripped her so tightly that she winced. He didn't seem to notice or care that he was hurting her.

His voice was strangled as he said, "Don't you ever, ever, ever run out on me—"

"But I didn't. I only—"

"Don't you even think about doing that," he said, his brown, almond-shaped eyes blazing with intensity.

"I won't," she said. "Oh, Chris...never, never again."

"Promise me, Annie," he said, almost with a sob, and touched his hands lightly to the bandage surrounding the crown of her head, as if suddenly just remembering her injury. "Promise me." He pressed her against him, hard, as if he might forcibly meld their bodies together.

"I pr—" But before she could finish, his lips had taken the words, her breath, her very heart away.

They slept together, holding each other tenderly. For once they did not make love.

"Headache," Chris said in explanation, when she was nestled into the crook of his arm.

Annie smiled and looked into his face, gauging what he was really feeling. He was tired. Their evening had been emotionally draining—for her, too. She tried to lighten the mood. "Are you kidding me? Isn't that supposed to be my line?"

He almost laughed, but stopped short.

Annie sensed that something still bothered him, but it was hard to know just what. For once in her life she found herself on the outside. She had never considered what it would be like to be shut out of his professional life, and it didn't feel good.

For hours she lay awake, troubled as Chris fell into a fitful sleep. Then, in spite of herself, she fell asleep.

When she awoke, it was morning and Chris was already dressed, ready to leave.

"Why didn't you wake me?" she asked, sitting up from the pillows and blinking her eyes free from sleep.

"It's good for you to rest." He was holding Muffin, and placed the cat in her arms.

Annie stroked the cat's fur. The resultant purr was a comforting sound in the silence.

"Don't forget, I'll be back around lunch to take you for your second session with Sandra Berkus."

"I'll be ready and waiting."

He studied her without speaking. "You'll be okay here? If not, I can call Jeff Parker's wife, and—"

"Yes, I'll be all right. Of course!" And she threw a pillow at him. "Go. Get out of here! Catch bad guys!"

He caught the pillow, then made a movement as if to leave, but stopped. "Just—don't let anyone in today, Annie."

"Okay—no one comes in."

"Not anyone."

"Okay, okay."

"See you," Chris said, left the room, then returned a second later to kiss her.

"Why won't you tell me what's wrong?" she asked him as he left the room the second time.

He hesitated, but didn't turn. "Maybe it's everything," he said, and kept on going.

Liz was more than happy to oblige him in his request.

"Well, you know, this is a funny coincidence. Hal and I were talking just last night—we both agree it's time to move on. You've done it, Chris—started over. And it was the right thing, of course. So," she said as she led him down the hall to the cabinet where the boxes of Laura's possessions had been placed, "you're really doing us a favor by going through these things. Take what you want, Chris. With our blessings. Hal and I talked about going through the stuff ourselves again, and just . . . just letting go."

Chris looked at his mother-in-law, slim and aristocratic in the tailored, blue silk shirtwaist dress. She was still a beautiful woman. There had always been something of Laura in her eyes, and he felt his heart race for a moment. "You've been good to me, Liz," he said suddenly with a passion that was inappropriate. He wished he could sit down with her and explain everything, ask her understanding, beg her forgiveness. But he couldn't.

"You've been good to me, Chris." Tears glistened in her eyes.

Chris nodded, then turned away. He hated himself.

It took him two trips to load the four boxes into the trunk of his car. On the last trip Liz accompanied him to the door. "Chris, next Thursday, how about roast duck in raspberry sauce? I know it made a big hit with you last September when the Greens came to dinner. You had three helpings." Liz was beaming. Her world was small and warm and simple. Laura's death had been, to Chris's knowledge, the only dark moment she had known in her life. Such innocence was a treasure to be protected. "Remember?" she coaxed playfully.

"I remember," he said, feeling his strength draining from his limbs.

"Raspberry duck, then?"

"That would be..." But he couldn't, not when he was destroying her small world even at that moment. "I'll call you, okay?"

And he hated himself more.

At the police department he began to sort through the stuffed animals, dolls, small glass perfume bottles—and finally found what he had been looking for.

In one of her earliest scrapbooks there was a perfectly clear clipping of Corrie Bonner. Years had passed, but it didn't matter. The angle and clarity of the photo made it possible to see the current likeness between yesterday's Bonner and today's.

And if there was anything that Hal Haverstrom had, it was vision.

Annie was dressed for her appointment. Chris would be coming for her about lunchtime, and they'd drive to Sandra Berkus's office at one o'clock.

She studied her reflection in the bathroom mirror. There wasn't much she could do about the bandages on her head, but she gave in to vanity and applied a bit of black mascara and some light blue shadow to her eyes.

She was on her way to the bedroom when the knocking sounded against the front door, followed by the bell.

Annie's initial impulse was to respond to the summons.

But then she remembered Chris's instructions not to open the door to anyone, and waited for the caller to leave. She felt strange, as if she were guilty of deception.

The pounding continued intermittently, along with the bell's insistence. The appeal finally stopped. The house pulsed with silence.

Curious, Annie crept quietly into the living room to peer out the front window.

Hal was striding down the drive heading toward the street. Chris had probably asked him to check on her.

His face lit up when she called to him from the open front door. He waved and walked rapidly back to the house.

"Thought I'd missed you," he said, trailing her into the living room. With his blue eyes he looked over her, taking her in with affection. "You look wonderful," he said. "I must say, you wear white gauze better than anyone I've ever seen."

Annie laughed. "Can I get you something? Tea? Coffee? A soft drink? Name it."

"Iced tea would be fine. No sugar."

Annie started into the kitchen. "When will Chris be here to get you?" Hal called from the living room.

"Oh, not for a while yet. An hour, soonest. I got ready early. You spoke to him this morning?"

"No. Not since yesterday. I called the office and they said he wasn't in, so I thought I'd stop by."

In the kitchen, Annie dropped a spoon, picked it up and dropped it again.

"You're nervous," Hal commented.

"Maybe. Oh, I guess so. Today's very important," she said from the kitchen.

"Understandable under the circumstances. A man's life depends upon what you remember."

Annie reached into the cupboard and took down two tall glasses. She placed them on the tiled counter and glanced back at Hal in the living room. He was watching her. He smiled when their eyes met, and she suddenly wanted to tell Hal about her past, wanted to confide in him about Corrie Bonner. Hal was like a father to her now, just as he was to Chris. It almost seemed wrong to hide things from him.

But he was asking her, "Do you think you'll recall anything that might help Chris?" and the moment of temptation passed.

"I think so. I want to," Annie said with feeling. And then, with increased assurance, she said, "Yes. I really think I will."

Opening the refrigerator, she scanned the interior for the container of iced tea she had seen before. She found it behind a milk carton, and pushing things aside, she drew out the glass pitcher.

She was just turning when she came smack against Hal. He had come up behind her so quietly that she hadn't heard him. With a quick gasp she tried to steady herself, but the tea sloshed in the pitcher and splashed against her wrist, then covered part of her bodice with a dark stain. She gave a small cry of despair, and in the next instant Hal grabbed her wrist to steady her.

The pitcher flew from her gasp and crashed to the floor.

"Sorry, oh sorry," she said, as it spilled against Hal's pants' cuffs. His grip was tight.

"You worry me, Annie," he said.

Dazed, she looked into ice blue eyes devoid of the former friendliness. For an instant she thought he wasn't Hal, but someone else.

"You're supposed to be resting, Annie. You've just escaped a serious injury, and look—you're overdoing things. See what happens?"

Nothing was making sense. The man before her was Hal, but suddenly he wasn't Hal. The eyes were cold, hard like steel. But the words...were they words of concern? Annie couldn't be sure. His hold on her was painful.

She tried to ease away.

But Hal pulled her back into him. His grip was firm and determined.

"Hal..." She struggled now, her heart starting to race as a genuine panic overwhelmed her. "Please...it hurts when you—"

Hal gave a yank. "Annie, you're overdoing things. You had a bad fall. You could get dizzy, could hit your head, anything could happen. Look," he said, "you've already dropped the pitcher."

"Hal, I...I don't know, but this doesn't seem...could you let go of my arm, please?"

The blue of his eyes bored into her. Behind them, sunlight poured in from the kitchen window over the sink, bleaching out the color and lines on one side of Hal's face.

Annie's eyes widened. There was something about the way the sun shone on his face.

And then she knew what it reminded her of. She saw it again—the man driving past her in the Ford...the hat...the profile...and that single, split second when he had looked to the side and his face was in sunlight, just as it was now.

The man had seen her; and she had seen him.

The man was Hal Haverstrom.

But the knowledge came too late.

Hal Haverstrom's grip grew stronger....

Chris stared at the picture of Corrie Bonner as he had looked twenty years before. He stared, but didn't see, his mind filled with incidents from his own life. Laura, his beautiful Laura, and Liz and Hal. Roast duck dinners and Christmas trees and grown-up Easter egg hunts where he'd find sentimental gifts in plastic eggs—and expensive trinkets from the Haverstroms tucked within green plastic grass beneath chocolate bunnies.

Laura. Liz. Hal. His family. He was the agent of their destruction.

Chris closed his eyes.

When he opened them, Jeff was standing in front of him with a folder, sheets of paper stuffed haphazardly between the covers as if placed there in a hurry. He didn't look any better than Chris felt. Their eyes met and held.

"I've got it," Jeff said. "What you didn't want."

Without expression, Chris took the folder from Jeff's hand and tossed it on the desk.

"Thanks. Excuse me a minute," he said, rising, and made his way quickly into the bathroom, where he vomited.

When he returned, Jeff was seated, his elbows on his knees, head between his hands.

He didn't move or say anything while Chris reviewed the data.

Every deal related to the canyon property was traced to companies owned by Hal Haverstrom. The companies were shells, corporations in name only. Over the years Haverstrom had been buying up land, parcel by parcel, until the only remaining parcel he didn't own was that belonging to the last victim.

It didn't take a wild leap of imagination to suspect that Hal's partner knew too much about Hal's enterprises, or that Hal simply didn't want to share his profits.

Likewise, the murdered bank appraiser had worked on several of the Haverstrom deals, and when he discovered the link between the dummy companies, he might have threatened to blow the whistle, or even to blackmail Hal. That could be checked out, as well.

As for the last victim, he wanted to hold on to the property, as symbolically it meant more to him than cash. It was "home." Hal got rid of him so he could pick up the property.

But he did it cleverly; Chris had to give him that, along with a badge for excellence in ruthlessness.

When Bonner had come to work there, Hal must have seen him. Coincidentally, having been going through Laura's things, he must have recognized Bonner from the picture. It was the perfect opportunity for Hal to get rid of the last remaining pawn in his bid to take over the canyon land, and if anyone was caught, it would be Corrie Bonner who was the most likely suspect, a man already wanted for murder.

Chris looked up.

Jeff shook his head and sighed. "Doesn't look good."

Chris just stared. It was too much to comprehend. Laura's father? What was he thinking?

He had been investigating the first murder case when he had met Laura. He hadn't been anywhere near Laura's league socially. But Laura had liked him, and Hal had seemed suddenly to thaw from his initial frozen attitude regarding their relationship to one of acceptance.

Then there had been the wildly attractive offer of a job with Hal's company, which would have pulled Chris off the case. He might have discovered Hal's involvement in the crime back then were it not that political pressures were exerted just at the crucial time, pressures that put Chris onto another investigation. For all Chris knew, Hal Haverstrom might have been instrumental in diverting the focus of his investigation. Hal had a lot of power, enough to influence a great many people.

"What can I do?" Jeff asked, his face filled with sympathy.

"Do?" Chris looked out the window. "You can tell me this is a bad dream."

At the sound of the front door opening, Hal dropped his hands and stepped back from Annie and turned as Chris moved into view.

There was a moment's hesitation as each man took in the other. Hal was the first to speak.

"Chris!" He started forward, then suddenly swung back around to Annie. "Don't worry about anything. Just easy, now . . . sit back down." He guided her to the chair by the kitchen table and eased her into it.

Annie's mind was racing as fast as her heart was beating, which was very fast. She could have been killed. Hal Haverstrom was a killer. She would tell Chris . . . tell Chris— "Chris!" she called.

Only her voice hardly sounded. Instead, the name came out as a raspy whisper, and already Hal was speaking, his voice smooth and deep and melodious.

"Chris is here . . ." Hal crooned comfortingly, as if to someone who was not quite right in the head. "I'm here . . . I think I'll call Liz." He began to turn, his eyes going toward the telephone. "If it's all right with Chris, that is—"

"If what's all right?" Chris stood in the kitchen doorway.

Annie stared at him. How was she going to tell him? Would he even believe her? What if she were mistaken—no, she wasn't.

Chris stared back at her, but his eyes were blank, his face grim.

Then he looked down. The shards of glass and spilled tea mingled in a puddle.

"Are you okay?" he asked, coming forward to Annie.

She nodded.

Hal broke in, his voice a deep well of concern. "She'll be fine, I'm sure," Hal said. "A bit of dizziness, I think. She was overdoing things, trying to play hostess. It's entirely my fault," he said energetically. "I shouldn't have let her. If you don't object, Chris, I'd like to call Liz and have her come over to stay with Annie. Maybe she could help out a bit while you're at work."

"No," Chris said, touching Annie's face softly with his hand. She looked into his face, and saw that he was staring down at the broken glass. "That won't be necessary." He met Annie's eyes again.

He looked different. She sensed sorrow and rage, perhaps even hate. She rubbed her arm, and Chris's eyes fell to the red mark on her wrist where Hal had gripped her.

"I suggest she stay home. I know you'd planned on the hypnosis session, Chris, but I think it might be better if you rescheduled it for another time." Hal spoke in a different tone now, in a confidential manner, the way people did when they were meaning to say more than they could in a third party's presence.

Chris nodded, looking from Hal to Annie. "I think you're right."

"No," Annie said. "I'm fine. I want to do it, Chris. I *want* to," she stressed, unwilling to allow Hal his small triumph, regardless of not needing a session. She remembered everything just fine. She met Hal's blue eyes across the space separating them; she could feel the hatred.

"Hal's right," Chris said. "I want you to rest."

"There you go," said Hal, smiling down at Annie.

She met his kindness with cold silence. The truth would come soon enough; instead of blurting everything out, though, she would need to sit down with Chris, to prepare him for the shock.

"I worry about you, Annie," Hal said kindly.

Annie rubbed her sore wrist. "I'm sure you do, Hal."

Hal understood. He smiled again lightly. It was his usual smile, one she had always assumed was genuine.

"Well, I'm going to be taking off now," Hal said. "Take good care of our girl," he said, nodding to Chris. Before he left, he put his hand on Annie's shoulder and gave her a fatherly pat. She shrugged his hand away.

But Chris didn't catch the moment between them; he was scrounging around under the sink for a paper bag in which to put the large pieces of glass.

"See you both for Thursday's dinner," Hal called just before leaving. "Liz says she's planning duck, this time...."

There was the sound of the door closing. Annie and Chris were finally alone.

She fought the sudden impulse to blurt out her terrible knowledge in one long breath, to have done with everything that was her responsibility and to leave Chris to deal with the legality and morality and calamity.

But of course she couldn't. She and Chris were as one. His pain would touch her all the same. For now it was still all hers—her knowledge, her pain. If she could only keep it to herself, she would. But life was never that simple.

Chris banished her to the living room while he cleaned up the kitchen. It was just as well, and she went without making a fuss about helping him. She needed the extra time alone to prepare herself.

She moved aimlessly around the living room, occasionally stopping to stare at something without seeing it.

How would it affect Chris to have to pull Laura's father in for murder? And how would he feel about her every time they made love, knowing that she was the one to have put him into the position of destroying the lives of people that he had loved and trusted?

And what if she just kept her mouth shut? Her heart leaped at the alternative. God only knew how many people had committed crimes and had never paid for them; the world continued to spin just the same.

Corrie Bonner would be released now that the facts were made clear about the Starstream crash. And she had already implicated a second man who had come by the house after Corrie had left. So Corrie was safely off the hook.

Yes. What if she just kept quiet about the rest?

She could hear Chris moving around in the kitchen. Such sweet domestic sounds, sweetness that would be shattered once she told him what she had seen.

But she had to let Chris know. If she didn't, then she would always be a threat to Hal Haverstrom, her own life in constant jeopardy.

Suddenly she closed her eyes. There was one last alternative. She could leave Laguna Beach. Then Chris wouldn't have to know the truth about Laura's father, and her own life would no longer be at risk.

Annie had a sudden picture of herself traveling down a highway, away from Chris. She winced in pain.

"What's wrong?" Chris's voice broke through the fantasy.

Annie opened her eyes, lifting her face to meet Chris's discerning brown eyes as he came toward her.

"Nothing," she said, letting his arms envelop her. With one hand he drew up her face, looking into it. His touch was gentle and masculine. She closed her eyes again and nestled her face against his chest. She smelled cologne and shuddered with desire. "It feels so good to be with you, Chris. It feels so right."

"I know. For me too." He moved his hand sensuously down her back, caressing her buttocks, and Annie felt his sudden hardening response against her pelvis.

Then there was a long, still silence.

"What's going on, Annie?" he whispered.

He was tense, expectant of her reply. And Annie knew that there would be no going back to the way things had been between them once she spoke.

Slowly, with hesitation, she drew herself apart from him, and examining his dark eyes for the answer, found it in her own self. She had to trust their love.

So without stopping, she told him what she had seen, what she had remembered.

"I'm sorry," she said, when she had finished.

Chris nodded, saying nothing. Then, moving listlessly, he went toward the small round table where a picture of Laura still remained.

"I didn't have any choice," she said weakly. "Like you said, it's the law. Something like that."

"Yeah, something like that." His eyes rested on her, two dark stains of sorrow obliterating her last hope that their love was stronger than the past he had shared with another woman and a family he loved.

He put the photograph down and left her to go into the bathroom. She heard tap water running and the sound of Chris splashing his face. Then he was back, moving toward the door with a blank expression that for some reason was far worse than hatred or pain or fury.

"No one else knows," she said, following his back with her eyes as he opened the door. "What you do with the information—that's your business." She sounded foolish, desperate. "Chris! I'm sorry!"

Chris looked over his shoulder to where she stood. His voice was hollow. "Annie, you can't imagine sorry... you can't even begin to know."

The door closed behind him, and she was alone, and very, very sorry, indeed. She was sorry for her whole life. And she was tired.

She lay on the bed, but didn't sleep. Every time she heard a sound, her heart would leap and she would hope it was Chris coming home to her. But it never was. A little before dawn she gave up her hopeless vigil. It was time to move on.

There were hardly any vehicles on the road as the sun began to rise. The Pacific was to her right, still gray and misty with early morning haze as she headed south on

Coast Highway toward the Mexican border. A van with some surfers had just pulled to the side of the road, bright yellow and blue and orange boards stacked on top of the vehicle. The scene would have made a nice painting.

It would have made a nice life, Laguna Beach.

When she got to San Diego, she would stop and pen Marge Briskin a line about how she had had to leave unexpectedly, and how she'd be in touch later. She'd say something vague, something about a sudden crisis and that she was sorry she couldn't have attended the gallery show, and that she would write to the foundation herself and tell them she wouldn't be able to accept their grant after all. She didn't want to be attached to anyone or anything; all she wanted was this, the open road before her.

She turned on the radio, tuning in a station that played Mexican music; but the song was sad and passionate and she was suddenly crying hard, her shoulders heaving, her foot pressed to the floor.

She didn't hear the siren. And she wouldn't have noticed the red flashing light behind her had she not glanced in her rearview mirror when she went to change lanes.

An unmarked police car was hot on her tail.

Perfect, Annie thought, slowing and pulling to the road's sandy shoulder. A nice fat speeding ticket was just what she needed. She was fishing for her registration in the glove compartment when her door was pulled open.

Starting, she turned quickly, holding out her license and registration. "I'm sorry if I was—"

She didn't have a chance to complete her sentence. Chris swung her out of the high seat and holding her tightly in his arms, said, "Don't you ever, ever run out on me again. Annie, if you ever—"

Then he was kissing her hard, and the two of them were crying.

"I had to," she tried to explain between kisses and tears. "I thought it was over...that you blamed me."

It was then that she saw Corrie. He was standing outside the unmarked car, an unclear silhouette against the brilliant dawn sky. He was watching them, and when he saw her look, he nodded. She thought he smiled; she couldn't be sure.

Chris looked down at her with love in his eyes. "It's a good thing he knows your habits. It saved me a lot of trouble finding you. He said you'd take the coast road and not the freeway." Chris paused. "How could you leave me, Annie?" He drew away slightly, wanting to see her more clearly.

"You didn't come home last night. Oh, Chris! I went mad. I thought it was over because I told you about Hal. I thought maybe what you had with them—with the Haverstroms—was something more solid than—"

"No," Chris said, looking heavenward, as if such a notion were utterly preposterous. "Nothing, Annie— nothing's more secure than my love for you. That's something it may take you a while to accept, but we've got a lot of time. As for your news, it wasn't any bombshell. The fact was, I already knew. It made me sick, of course. But I just needed to confirm a few things. Then, when I came home and saw Hal there..." Chris ran his fingers through his hair. Shaking his head, he said, "I've got to tell you, I was shaken. I could have lost you. And it would have been my fault for not moving faster. I should have sat down and talked to you then, but I was too freaked out by what might have happened if I hadn't have come by when I did. I had to do something, had to act, get finished with the whole mess.

"The bad stuff's over for us, Annie. There's never going to be another reason for you to run down any other highway again. That's a promise." He scooped her into his arms again, and she could feel his heart beating in time with her own. "Hal's signed a full confession," Chris said. "He wanted to spare Liz a trial, all the publicity."

"Is she okay?" Annie asked.

"It's hard for her to understand, but she loves him. He loves her, too. Strange, isn't it? Love leading to murder. He said he always wanted to be the best for her and Laura, to see that they had the best of everything. He let his need to be number one in everything run off with his judgment. And Liz..." Chris sighed. "Liz just cried when the truth came tumbling out, and she said that all she ever wanted or needed was his love. She's going to stand by him."

Chris had Corrie drive his car back to the station. They would take the Volkswagen bus.

"I want to drive," she insisted. "For the first time, I'm taking the highway home," she said.

They drove together in silence with Muffin curled in the back of the van and Corrie a few car lengths before them. The emerging day was turning golden on the horizon. The mist had lifted completely.

* * * * *

COMING NEXT MONTH

#595 TEA AND DESTINY—Sherryl Woods
Ann Davies had always taken in strays—but never one as wild as playboy
Hank Riley! She usually offered tea and sympathy, but handsome Hank
seemed to expect a whole lot more....

#596 DEAR DIARY—Natalie Bishop
Adam Shard was falling hard for his childhood pal. But beneath the
straightforward, sardonic woman Adam knew so well lay a Kerry Camden
yearning for love...and only her diary knew!

#597 IT HAPPENED ONE NIGHT—Marie Ferrarella
When their fathers' comedy act broke up, impulsive Paula and straitlaced
Alex grudgingly joined forces to reunite the pair. But after much muddled
meddling by everyone concerned, it was hard to say exactly *who* was
matchmaking whom...

#598 TREASURE DEEP—Bevlyn Marshall
A sunken galleon, a tropical isle and dashing plunderer Gregory Chase...
Could these fanciful fixings finally topple Nicole Webster's decidedly
*un*romantic theory on basic biological urges?

#599 STRICTLY FOR HIRE—Maggi Charles
An accident brought unwanted luxury to take-charge Christopher
Kendall's fast-paced life—a lady with a limo! And soon bubbly,
rambunctious, adorable Tory Morgan was driving him to utter
amorous distraction!

#600 SOMETHING SPECIAL—Victoria Pade
With her pink hearse, her elderly companion and her dubious past, there
was something mighty suspicious about Patrick Drake's new neighbor,
beautiful Mitch Cuddy. Something suspicious, something
sexy...something pretty damn special !

AVAILABLE THIS MONTH:

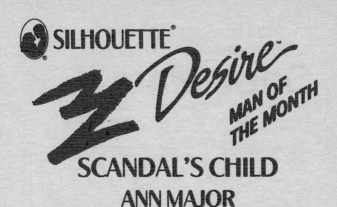

SCANDAL'S CHILD
ANN MAJOR

When passion and fate intertwine...

Garret Cagan and Noelle Martin had grown up together in the mysterious bayous of Louisiana. Fate had wrenched them apart, but now Noelle had returned. Garret was determined to resist her sensual allure, but he hadn't reckoned on his desire for the beautiful scandal's child.

Don't miss SCANDAL'S CHILD by Ann Major, Book Five in the Children of Destiny Series, available now at your favorite retail outlet.
